NOT QUITE A LADY

Caroline Brooke is bereft when her father dies, leaving her his fortune. Whilst trying to cope with running her father's estate she attracts the interest of two admirers — sophisticated Edward Seymour and Robert Parker, a blunt-speaking mill master. Seymour offers her security in a world she knows and understands, whilst Parker challenges her long-held beliefs. But when she discovers a devastating secret, which threatens her heritage and reputation, how can she consider the attentions of either?

Books by Angela Drake
in the Linford Romance Library:

STAY VERY CLOSE

ANGELA DRAKE

◆

NOT QUITE A LADY

Complete and Unabridged

LINFORD
Leicester

First published in Great Britain in 2006

First Linford Edition
published 2007

British Library CIP Data

Drake, Angela
    Not quite a lady.—Large print ed.—
Linford romance library
    1. Love stories
    2. Large type books
    I. Title
    823.9'14 [F]

ISBN 978–1–84617–828–3

Published by
F. A. Thorpe (Publishing)
Anstey, Leicestershire

Set by Words & Graphics Ltd.
Anstey, Leicestershire
Printed and bound in Great Britain by
T. J. International Ltd., Padstow, Cornwall

This book is printed on acid-free paper

1

Dinner was over and it was time for the ladies to withdraw. Nodding to the gentleman they filed out of the dining-room in a rustle of silk and gentle murmurings. Their departure was closely observed by two of the men in the company, watchful until the elegantly coiffured head of their hostess, Caroline Brooke, had passed out of sight. They glanced swiftly at each other; two young men who had not met before, yet were instantly aware that a seed of rivalry had planted itself between them.

One of these young men was Robert Parker, a newcomer and a rising young manufacturer in the district. The request to dine at the country house of the great landowner and industrialist, Arthur Brooke, had come as something of a surprise. It was only recently that

Robert had chanced to meet Brooke while visiting a textile exhibition.

The older man had introduced himself and talked for a while of the ingenious new techniques being introduced in the weaving trade. It had never crossed Robert's mind that the renowned entrepreneur's casual, 'I hope we shall have the pleasure of welcoming you at Brackenfield some day,' would be closely followed by a formal invitation printed on thick vellum.

He watched with interest as Brooke, silver-haired and commanding, now rose to his feet and invited his guests to join him in drinking to the health of his Majesty the King. The toasts completed, Brooke set the conversational ball rolling. 'Gentlemen, whilst the ladies chatter about their new gowns and the vexations of keeping the servants in order, we men must attempt to put the world to rights!'

Having ushered the ladies into the cream and gold drawing-room, Caroline Brooke settled herself in the corner of a sofa and reflected that the evening was turning out to be a success. The menu she had planned with Cook had turned out excellently and she was sure that the guests were enjoying themselves.

Beside her on the sofa was her widowed aunt, Hilda Forsett, who was observing Miss Amelia Derby as she played a minuet on piano whilst Mrs Derby turned the pages of the music. Leaning towards Caroline, Aunt Hilda whispered in her ear, 'One can hardly say that Miss Derby gets any more beautiful as the months go by. It's a good thing her father plans to settle a sizeable fortune on her when she marries. What man would have her otherwise?'

'Aunt Hilda!' warned Caroline. She loved her aunt, but had noticed that as the years went by her father's sister had become increasingly outspoken and provocative.

'She shouldn't wear red,' her aunt continued, 'it simply emphasises the shade of her nose. She should take a leaf out of your book, my dear, and wear blue. So much more becoming!'

Caroline sighed. She stood up and went to ask Mrs Derby if she would like more coffee.

'No more coffee, Miss Brooke,' Mrs Derby said in her blunt, commanding way. 'I have been wanting to ask you if your young Mr Seymour is a business colleague of Mr Brooke's. I didn't quite gather what his occupation is. Is the gentleman new in this district?'

'He is to be our new neighbour at Kelshaw Hall,' Caroline told her.

'Really!' Mrs Derby's eyes sharpened with speculation.

'He's the nephew of Mr Grimshaw who died last summer,' Caroline elaborated. 'Mr Grimshaw bequeathed Mr Seymour the house and the estate.'

'So Mr Seymour must have come into a considerable fortune,' Mrs Derby said thoughtfully.

'I believe so,' said Caroline, fancying she could almost hear the sound of gold coins clinking in Mrs Derby's head as she estimated Seymour's wealth.

'And does he have a wife?' Mrs Derby queried.

'Not to my knowledge,' Caroline said mischievously. A picture of the elegant Mr Seymour sprang into her mind. She could understand the matron's flutter of interest. Mr Seymour was certainly eligible, a man with undeniable charm; blond locks, an athletic figure and more than his fair share of good looks.

'And Mr Parker?' continued Mrs Derby. 'I haven't come across him before.'

'Mr Parker is the owner of Parker Mills just a few miles south of here,' Caroline said evenly. 'He hasn't been in the area long. We know little about him as yet.'

'Well, I can tell you that Mr Parker has no wife,' Aunt Hilda announced. 'I asked him straight out, and he answered straight back. He is not a man to trifle with, I fancy. He has very fine eyes under those grim black brows, but I daresay he would not be to every young lady's taste.'

Caroline groaned inwardly. She wondered what Robert Parker would think if he could hear himself being discussed as a potential catch for marriageable young ladies. Talking with him before dinner she had found him a touch serious, but perfectly agreeable. Not a charmer, but a man you could trust.

In the dining-room, Robert was becoming increasingly uneasy as the conversation turned to the issue of the mill workers' resistance to the new machinery which would revolutionise the output of cloth. Resistance which had led to violent break-ins at local mills in order to destroy the feared machines.

Mr Hugh Derby, Amelia's father and an established and wealthy mill-owner in the locality had firm views on the matter. 'I'll make my cloth by what means I choose,' he said, his face grim.

There were murmurs of approval. Robert sat quiet and still, pondering his contributions to this discussion, knowing that he must speak with care.

'Who are these saboteurs — where do they come from?' enquired the young man who had shared Robert's interest in watching Caroline lead the ladies out of the dining-room. The gentleman in whom Mrs Derby had shown such eager curiosity. 'You must forgive me,' he said with a lazy smile, 'I have only just come up from London to the north and I'm woefully ignorant about the textile trade.'

'Well then, Mr Seymour,' Arthur Brooke responded, 'I must enlighten you. For your information sir, most of the vandals here in Yorkshire, and nearby Lancashire, are weavers. Men who have spent their lives at the hand loom.'

'And now they see machines taking over their livelihood?' suggested Seymour.

'Precisely.'

'Surely they can get work tilling the land or keeping pigs,' Seymour drawled.

Guffaws of approval ran around the table.

Robert drew in a breath. 'It is hard for a mill hand to be laid off when he has no other means of buying bread for his family than the payments for his work at the loom,' he observed steadily.

All eyes focused on him. Who was this young newcomer amongst them who dared to take the side of the workers and to challenge the wisdom of their collective experience?

Brooke leaned forward, frowning in displeasure. 'Mr Parker, as a mill master just starting up in business you must learn the importance of keeping your workers under firm control. Take your cue from those of us who have years of dealing with working folk.'

'I did not mean to give offence, sir,' Robert told him. 'I merely offered an opinion about the plight of my weavers should powered machines replace the old hand looms.'

'Which, of course they will,' exclaimed Brooke impatiently. 'In manufacturing one cannot afford to stand still; that way lies stagnation and bankruptcy. Surely you cannot disagree with that?'

'No sir,' Robert agreed courteously. 'I certainly cannot.'

'Have you no thoughts of installing power looms in your own mill?' Brooke enquired. 'For if you resist mechanisation you will be ruined, Mr Parker, a pauper without means or occupation.'

There was a roar of delighted laughter. Edward Seymour leaned back in his chair, his eyes gleaming with satisfaction to see this earnest fellow Parker put in his place.

'I have already installed four machines,' Robert said quietly. 'But I still find it hard to look on whilst my mill hands are thrown out of work.'

'Let me assure you,' Brooke said, 'that some of them will have no qualms about damaging your interests. They will be out for themselves. Every working man has the potential for being a scheming Luddite and machine wrecker.'

'No! I cannot accept that, sir,' Robert protested, unable to stop himself. 'That is not the truth.'

A spasm of intense feeling distorted Brooke's features. 'You call me a liar, sir? In my own house?' he hissed. 'I demand an apology!'

'It was not my intention to cause you displeasure, sir,' Robert assured him in consternation.

'Apologise!' shouted Brooke, jumping to his feet, the veins on his forehead standing out like ropes. 'My God, Parker, I thought you were one of us. That we would share a common interest as civilised entrepreneurs and mill masters. Yet you take my hospitality and then presume to insult me.'

Robert's mouth dried, his voice became locked in his throat.

'So!' Brooke cried. 'You refuse to offer me an apology. By God, my father would have called you out over an insult such as this! Leave my house, Mr Parker. Now, this minute.'

Dismayed, Robert rose to his feet. He

judged there was no way of retrieving the situation at this stage. Yet to offer an apology on Brooke's terms was unthinkable. He had been guilty of nothing except maintaining his own point of view in a respectful manner.

As he prepared to leave the room he thought again of Caroline Brooke, and the welcome she had offered him as the guests were assembling. How she had jested a little, drawing him out and making him feel more of a man than he could remember any woman having done for some time. But maybe she was just a flirt. He'd experienced plenty of those. Yet somehow he had believed in her, had felt himself enlivened and warmed by her presence.

On impulse he turned from the door and walked towards Arthur Brooke in the hope of wishing him a civil goodnight. There was not a sound in the room, only the soft hiss of burning candlegrease.

Brooke took a step back. His eyes suddenly flared with renewed rage. 'Do you dare to approach me sir! Ho! Leave this instant before I get my servants to throw you out!' Snatching up the silver-handled cane beside his chair he raised it in the air, causing Robert to throw up his arm in an automatic gesture of self defence.

For a long time afterwards Robert found it hard to recall precisely what happened. There were shots from the other men. 'Shame on him! Strike the fellow! Give him his just deserts!' And then there was the sting of the cane as it brushed his earlobe, heating the flesh. He vaguely recollected raising his hand higher, pushing it outwards to fend off further blows. And then he was striding through the hallway, heading for the front door.

Unaware of the events in the dining-room, Aunt Hilda was happily airing her views on the benefits of marriage. 'I keep telling my dear niece that it is high time she started thinking about marriage,' she announced. 'But I suspect she doesn't agree with me.'

'That's not so,' Caroline countered. 'I do sometimes think about marriage — as a possibility for the future.'

'Well, my dear,' said Aunt Hilda, 'I can understand that you are happy to be mistress of this gracious house, and to act as hostess to your father's guests, but you must think seriously of the future.' She turned to the company. 'Caroline was a girl of fourteen when her mother died, you know, and she had to take on the responsibilities of the lady of the house. My brother couldn't have wished for a more dutiful daughter.'

'I couldn't agree with you more on the subject of an early marriage,' Mrs Derby said. 'That is exactly what I keep telling Amelia. But young ladies these days seem to think they know better than those of us with experience of life.' She looked pointedly at Caroline as she spoke.

'I would like to marry one day,' Caroline said with gentle conviction. 'But as far as I can see, there must be only a very few men in the world that I would want to spend my life with. For a start they must come up to all the standards my father has taught me to expect of a man. They must be sincere and steadfast and loyal. They must be loving and tender too. And brave, amusing and witty. And so on, and so on.' Her eyes sparkled impishly. 'How will I find such a paragon?'

'Now, Caroline,' chided Aunt Hilda. 'I think you are simply mocking us with playful jests.'

'Not at all,' said Caroline firmly, bringing the topic to a close. She was just thinking it was high time the gentlemen joined them when there were was the thud of feet marching through the hallway. Alarmed, Caroline excused herself and ran out to see what was amiss. She was astonished to see Robert Parker striding down the hallway to the door, his dark brows drawn together and an expression of thunderous displeasure on his face.

'Mr Parker, sir!' she exclaimed.

He turned to meet her gaze, his dark

eyes on fire with a strange, pent up emotion.

There was a tense silence as Caroline stared at him, at a loss to know what to think. 'Are you leaving us, sir?' she asked.

'Yes. I'm afraid . . . ' He stopped, pressing his lips together.

'Without saying goodnight?' she enquired, unable to conceal her disapproval at such bad manners.

'Yes. I believe I must go without delay,' he said stiffly. 'I am sorry. Goodnight, Miss Brooke.'

As he shut the front door behind him she felt a waft of freezing night air and gave an involuntary shiver. She stood very still for a moment, not quite able to believe that Mr Parker had left in such a manner, with no words of explanation or a proper farewell. Indeed she could not recall any guest at Brackenfield having departed in such a rude and unceremonious manner.

Edward Seymour sauntered through into the hallway. 'Ah, Miss Brooke!'

'Is there anything amiss?' Caroline asked in concern.

'No, no. All is well, ma'am!' There was something teasing and indulgent in the way he was looking at her. Caroline was annoyed to find herself disconcerted. 'Where are the footmen?' she asked crisply. 'They should be here when a guest leaves.'

'You don't need the footmen to tell you what has been happening Miss Brooke,' Seymour informed her smoothly. 'I can tell you all you want to know. There has simply been a slight irritation to deal with.' He paused. 'Mr Parker was asked to leave.'

'I beg your pardon. Asked to leave?' She was astonished.

'Yes. And he has now done just that.'

'But why?'

'Your father found it necessary to suggest that he remove himself.'

Caroline tried, but failed, to visualise the scene. 'Oh, good heavens! I can't believe it. Mr Parker seemed such a measured gentleman.'

Seymour raised an eyebrow. 'You may be surprised to hear that Parker has very definite and somewhat revolutionary views. He stirred up a bitter argument with your father.'

'Really!' Caroline stared at Edward Seymour in bewilderment.

'Your father was very forebearing, but there comes a time when even the most tolerant man's patience snaps. You see, instead of backing down graciously Parker would insist on forcing his views down your father's throat,' Seymour added with regret.

'Oh, surely not!'

'Your father endured Parker's tirade with great restraint. But, in the end, when the fellow branded your father a liar he had no choice but to ask him to apologise — or be on his way.'

'Mr Parker refused the opportunity to apologise!' Caroline exclaimed in horror.

'I'm afraid it's true,' Seymour told her. 'You need only ask your father.'

'Oh, poor Papa!' exclaimed Caroline.

'What an unpleasant thing to have happened.'

At that point she saw her father emerge from the dining-room, and hurried forward. 'Dear Papa. I am so sorry to hear of the difficulty you have just been through.'

'I think it is the very first time I have had to ask a guest to leave Bracken-field,' he told her, his voice grave. 'And I hope it will be the last.'

She took his arm as they made their way to the drawing-room. She noticed that his steps were uncharacteristically slow and deliberate, and when she looked into his face she saw that it was set and grim, as though he were in pain, a spike of alarm shot through her nerves.

The ladies in the drawing-room were trying to pretend nothing untoward had happened, although as Caroline guided her father through the door she could sense the silent speculations.

Brooke settled himself in a chair beside the fire and spoke to the

anxious-looking guests. 'Please everyone, I assure you nothing is amiss.
Caroline, my dear, why not send for
fresh tea and coffee? And Miss Derby,
how about a song before it's time for us
all to say goodnight?'

He was smiling and commanding,
back to his old self. But Caroline could
hear a slight falter in his voice, an old
man's quaver she had never heard before.

When at last the final carriage had
rolled away, she knelt down beside his
chair and laid her hand on his arm.
'What can I do to make my favourite
person in the world look happier?' she
asked softly.

'Just be here and be yourself, my
dear.' He stroked her hair, his fingers
moving slowly over the gleaming
chestnut strands.

'Will you talk to me about what
happened tonight?' she asked.

'No,' he responded sharply. 'I've no
wish to rake over the distressing scenes
that occurred.'

'Talking sometimes takes the pain

out of the memory of bad events.'

He gave an indulgent smile. 'How did you learn such wisdom in your short life my dear?'

'I learned a good deal after Mama died. You and I used to take long walks and talk about the happy times before she became ill. Sharing our sorrow seemed to make the hurting less.'

'Yes,' he said, 'I remember.' He sighed and a sudden spasm of pain contorted his features. 'I don't think I want to talk just now. You must forgive me, my dear.'

Caroline grasped his hands within hers. 'Oh Papa, what is there to forgive you for? Do let me get you something: a little brandy perhaps?'

'Yes, my dear. I think that would be very acceptable.'

Caroline went into the dining-room and poured a measure of brandy into a glass. When she got back to the drawing-room her father had fallen asleep, his head slumped against his chest. She shook him gently. 'Wake up,

Papa. Here's your brandy.'

His eyes seemed blurred and vacant as though he had been in the deepest sleep.

'Perhaps I should ask Laidlaw to come and help you to bed,' Caroline said.

Her father shook himself like a dog getting up from its bed after a night's sleep. 'No, no. I'll go up later. I'm quite all right now, my dear.'

He sipped his brandy and they chatted for a while about their plans to visit friends in Scotland in the spring. He really did seem much brighter.

Eventually Caroline felt happy to say goodnight to him, confident that all was now well again. When he had got over the shock of what had happened she was sure that he would want to confide in her. She bent to kiss his forehead. He took her hand. 'You are the most precious gift God gave me,' he said suddenly, both touching and surprising her, as he did not make a habit of expressing his feelings.

'And so are you, Papa,' she responded softly. She turned to leave him. She heard him murmur something.

'Papa?'

'Nothing, my dear, nothing.'

Caroline closed the door softly behind her and crept away. She would have been concerned to hear his low moan of pain - far more concerned to hear him calling out a name she had never heard him speak before.

2

The rain clouds had lifted, leaving the night-sky clear and still. Reaching the highroad, Robert let his horse settle into a steady trot in preparation for the five-mile ride to his house on the southern outskirts of Bradford. He found himself unable to shake off the jagged memories of the evening. He kept recalling the way in which Arthur Brooke's refined features had distorted into ugliness as the dispute between them had escalated.

He still could not quite understand why things had turned out so badly. Clearly the topic of the workers had touched a raw nerve with Arthur Brooke.

And then Robert's thoughts turned to himself; the humiliation he had suffered. The memory of it brought out a prickle of heat beneath his necktie as he imagined the displeasure on Caroline Brooke's face as she listened to the accounts of what had happened. It was not hard to guess what Miss Brooke's opinion of him would be at this moment.

He decided to turn off the road, calculating that a short cut through the fields would shorten his journey by around twenty minutes. Putting his horse into a canter he allowed her to let off some high spirits in jumping hedges and walls. Soon he could make out the shape of his house, its high gable and stack of tall chimneys silhouetted against the sky. And beyond the house the broad hulk of the mill.

With a stab of alarm he registered a chink of light showing through one of the windows. He never left candles burning in the mill, the danger of fire being a harsh reality in a building filled with oily fleeces and floating fibres.

Thieves had broken in. Would they be in the counting house, looking for money? No, he didn't think so.

Everyone in the area knew that his money-safe was as strong as a fortress. No, it would not be his money, but his new looms the intruders were after.

Putting the horse into a gallop, he raced down the grassy slope and into the mill yard. The large sooty flank of the mill towered above him. All seemed quiet, but it was too dark to see if any windows were smashed or the entry doors forced.

Dismounting, he led the horse into his stall then, holding a lighted lantern, made his way to the entrance of the mill his mind filled with images of the terrible destruction which might be waiting for him. Cautiously he pulled open the entry doors, made his way to the main weaving shed and looked around him.

The intruders had gone, but their work was instantly apparent. Robert's four new steam-powered looms lay in pieces on the floor, a single candle burning amongst the debris of smashed iron frames, slashed wooden struts and brutally ripped cloth.

His dismay began to escalate as he calculated the implications of the vandalism. The ruined machines had been costly and he had risked a sizeable proportion of his available capital to buy them. But not only that, his order books were full and he had been relying on the amazing speed of these machines to produce and deliver huge quantities of cloth within a very short period of time. Now he would have to go back on his promises. Earnings would be lost, his reputation badly dented.

As he stared around him, his eye suddenly caught the gleam of something white attached to one of the pillars supporting the shed's lofty ceiling. Reaching out he found a folded sheet of torn paper, stained with sooty finger marks. He opened it out. There was no address or date, just a message. It had obviously been written by a man with no formal education, and Robert had to look twice to make out the meaning of some of the words.

To Mr Parker — Master of Parker Mills,

Your meesheens is all pulled down and cut into bits. This is a warnin from men that is starvin and have starving wifes and childer to go home to. You are a damd infernol dog, Master Parker, and beefor Almighty God we will pull down all the mill and cut out your damd heart if you get more new meesheens. If you get them you shall Hear from us again. Beware.

Robert folded the paper and slipped it in his pocket. And you shall hear from me if I find out who you are, he thought grimly. The irony of what had been happening in his mill whilst he had been championing the workers' cause at Brackenfield was not lost on him.

When Caroline woke the next morning, the sun was pouring into the room. Overhead the sky was a deep cobalt blue.

27

She stretched, deciding that it was a perfect morning for a ride out through the Brackenfield estate. She would persuade her father to go with her. The exercise and fresh air would do him good. As she lay making plans, she became aware of a low murmur of voices on the landing outside her room. She was suddenly seized with some strange alarm.

She swung her legs out of bed and shrugged on a long silk robe over her nightgown. As she opened the door, she saw that her maid, Susan, was already standing behind it, her hand raised, but frozen into immobility as if she could not summon up courage to knock.

'What is it Susan?' Caroline asked.

Susan licked her lips. 'Oh, Miss Brooke.' She paused, her eyes wide and scared-looking. 'Mr Laidlaw has sent me specially to fetch you. He must speak to you as soon as possible. He's in Mr Brooke's dressing room.'

Caroline was seized with alarm. 'My father!' she exclaimed. 'Is he ill?'

'Yes, ma'am.'

Caroline took a deep breath and tried to get a grip on her confused feelings. Pushing back her hair, which was loose and flowing around her shoulders, she ran the length of the landing and burst into her father's dressing room. Mr Laidlaw, the senior servant in the household, was standing by the window, staring out into the garden. He turned to face her.

'Miss Brooke,' he said quietly. 'I am deeply sorry to tell you that when I took the tea into your father a few minutes ago, I found him on the floor of his room.'

'He has had a collapse?' Caroline asked wildly.

'Yes, ma'am,' Laidlaw said carefully. 'I believe he had some sort of collapse. I have already sent for Doctor Lawrence.'

'Thank you.' She turned swiftly towards the door of the bedroom. 'I shall go and see my father. We shouldn't leave him on his own.'

As she reached for the door handle, Laidlaw called out to her. 'Perhaps you should wait until the doctor has been and we have moved him, ma'am.'

Caroline swivelled round, her face now pale with dread. 'Mr Brooke is dead, ma'am,' Laidlaw said.

The room seemed to shiver and pitch like a boat on a stormy sea. 'No,' she moaned. 'No!'

'I am very sorry, ma'am,' Laidlaw intoned with formal correctness.

'I shall go to him,' Caroline said, bracing herself for what she would find. Her heart beat painfully as she went into the bedroom and saw the hunched body of her father lying on the floor beside the bed, a coverlet thrown over him so that only his head was visible.

Slowly, hesitantly she bent down and touched his cheek with the tips of her fingers. The stiff, waxy coldness of his skin sent waves of shock through her nerves.

There was a little cough behind her. Laidlaw had slipped silently into the room, and was now standing respectfully at a distance behind her. Through her grief and panic-stricken disbelief she realised that she was now the true mistress of the house. In fact both master and mistress.

She got to her feet, determined to maintain a calm and dignified front. 'Please summon all the servants, Laidlaw,' she said. 'I shall speak to them in half-an-hour.'

In her dressing room, she stood resigned and numbed with grief as Susan helped her into a gown of black silk, wound a black ribbon through her hair and hung a string of grey pearls around her neck.

She viewed herself in the long cheval mirror. The sombre gown, the severity of her coiffure and the simplicity of her adornments seemed to have settled a strange, quiet calm on her. When Dr Lawrence arrived she was able to greet him with a composed dignity remarkable for a young woman who had just suffered a terrible and shocking blow.

Dr Lawrence was not a man to mince

words. 'Your father has suffered a seizure, Miss Brooke,' he informed her briskly. 'He has been dead for some hours.'

'Did he suffer?' Caroline asked.

'With seizures in the brain consciousness is soon lost. The patient feels very little.'

'What could have caused my father to be taken ill so suddenly?' she asked, determined to know the truth.

Dr Lawrence frowned. 'Sadly as I did not see your father before the event I am not able to answer that question. However, eminent members of my profession have noted that seizures can sometimes occur after undue exertion, or excitement. It is hard to be more precise.'

'I see.' Caroline stared down at her hands, speculative and troubled.

When the doctor had left she asked Laidlaw if he would arrange for the news of her father's death to be communicated first to her Aunt Hilda, and then to friends, neighbours, and

running in first. It was a minute past six o'clock and the winter dawn was just beginning to replace the night, penetrating the icy darkness with a pale translucent glow.

Every window in the mill was lit up and the mill bell was clanging loudly. The children were in a rush, afraid of being late. Robert counted them as they ran by. He gave the straggling latecomers a quiet reprimand, knowing that it would be repeated much more sharply by Jim Stott, the overlooker, once they reached the work-rooms.

But Robert would not permit coarseness or cruelty in his mill, no child was ever struck or flogged, which was not the case in many other work places.

By ten o'clock a large red sun had risen and the overlookers gave the signal for refreshment and a rest of half-an-hour for all the work hands. The children came out from gathering up the fluff from under the looms and skipped about enjoying their freedom.

It was Robert's custom to arrange for

hot coffee to be on offer each morning, and the children ran to find the little tin cans they had brought from home so as to hold them beneath the spout of the big urn set on a long low table. After that they collected their allowance of fresh bread which had been piled into small baskets lined up at the end of the table.

When he was satisfied that all was proceeding smoothly, Robert left the mill-yard and walked along to his house. It was a large house for one person and two creaky old servants, but he had had no choice about buying as it had been included in the sale of the mill as an inseparable lot. A light lunch had been laid out for him in the dining room but he was not hungry.

Throwing his riding coat over his arm he mounted up and set out towards the town, a ride which would take around half-an-hour. As he approached the cluster of shops and factories and offices he noted the grey haze hanging over the city; the smell of smoke and soot in the air. In the city centre, ragged, grey-faced children crawled in and out of doorways, or screamed from inside. Lumbering wagons clattered along carrying bales of cloth from the warehouses.

Stopping outside a tall building with several brass plates on the door he took the steps up to the third floor and knocked on the door bearing the name of Samuel Jacobson, Cloth Merchant.

Mr Jacobson, a balding man in his forties, sat at his desk, poring over a pile of papers. The desk was otherwise bare apart from a set of gleaming brass scales for weighing coins. Two or three token rolls of cloth leaned against the wall. Selling cloth was no longer Jacobson's main occupation.

'Ah, Mr Parker!' Jacobson exclaimed, his eyes sharp and knowing. 'What can I do for you?'

Robert sat down and delivered his news without preamble. 'I had visitors at Parker Mill last night. My four new power looms were smashed to pieces.'

'I see,' Jacobson said gravely. 'And do

you know who these 'visitors' were?'

'Not as yet, but I shall make every effort to find out. My immediate concern is to replace the machine without delay.' His voice was low and heavy with concern.

'And you would like my assistance?' Jacobson gave the smile of a cat anticipating cream.

'I don't believe I can do very much without it, Mr Jacobson,' Robert said. 'My profits over recent years have all been ploughed back into the business.

'You will need another loan of the same amount as the last one? On the same terms?'

Robert steeled himself. 'I will need around half as much again. As you know I used a substantial amount of my ready capital for the purchase of these last four machines.'

Jacobson nodded sagely. 'With a secondary loan I shall require a rate of interest fifteen per cent higher than that agreed for the previous advance. I hope that will be acceptable?'

Robert swallowed. 'Yes. That will be acceptable.'

'Now — I wonder what you can offer me as security.' Jacobson made a show of considering. 'Given your current situation, sir, I'm thinking I shall have to suggest that you assign the house.'

The house assigned and at risk! That was a blow for Robert. But at least Jacobson had not required a portion of the mill. To put the mill at risk of being taken from him would have been too hard to bear.

'And also the mill house,' Jacobson said softly.

Robert flinched. He considered getting up and walking out. But what alternatives had he? 'Very well,' he agreed. 'When will the money be available?' He held his breath.

Jacobson smiled. 'As soon as you want it, my friend.' He rustled amongst his pile of papers. 'If you will be kind enough to sign this pledge of payment for me now, we can conclude the rest of the paperwork later.'

The advance of the loan is so swift, Robert thought grimly, and the payment is so long and hard. He stood up and reached for his hat. 'Thank you for your help, Mr Jacobson.'

'Not at all,' said Mr Jacobson, silkily. He held the door open for Robert. 'Oh, by the way, have you heard the sad news about Mr Arthur Brooke?'

Robert stopped abruptly, his heart taking a painful leap. 'News! No. What news?'

'He died in the night. A brain seizure apparently. I heard about it from one of my earlier clients. I should think the news will be all over the town by now.'

Recalling the angry scenes of the night before, Robert was filled with dismay. Had Brooke already been ill during the dinner? Had he been in that delicate state where any disturbance or excitement could push him to the edge of the precipice? Had he, Robert, been the one to nudge him closer to that edge?

Brooke dead. He could hardly believe

it. And Caroline Brooke left with no parent to guide or support her. 'Oh, poor Miss Brooke,' Robert exclaimed impulsively.

'The lady is to be pitied in her sorrow,' Jacobson agreed. 'But poor, I don't think so.'

The merchant's sly innuendo grated. Nodding curtly Robert slammed his hat down on his head and walked swiftly away.

Riding back to the mill his thoughts were filled with the news of Brooke's death and a growing uneasiness that he, Robert, was somehow implicated in it. If only he had backed down when Brooke became agitated, if only he had given the apology that was asked for, however unfair the demand.

He kept recalling the carefree smiles with which Caroline Brooke had greeted him the night before. And then his imagination threw up a picture of how she must be now, her face pale and heavy with sorrow. He had an over-whelming impulse to ride on to

Brackenfield and see for himself how she was faring. But being a sensible man, he returned to his mill.

Edward Seymour had no such reservations about calling on Caroline without delay. Having announced his presence to Laidlaw he strode into the drawing room and swept her a low bow.

She looked white and drawn and her large blue eyes brimmed with tears as he offered eloquent condolences. 'Perhaps I should leave you, ma'am, and return at a later date,' he suggested courteously.

'No, please stay. There is a certain matter you can help me with, sir.' She paused, fighting back the waves of misery which were constantly sweeping over her.

'You have only to ask,' he said.

'This is a delicate matter. I've been thinking a good deal about the evening before my father died. About the . . . discussion he had with Mr Parker.'

'Disagreement,' Seymour interposed. 'A dispute, in fact. About the issue of certain scoundrels who are going around the county breaking into mills and smashing up the new power machinery.'

'Yes, quite. I know from my father about the serious threat these men pose to manufacturers.' She sighed. 'How serious was this . . . dispute?'

'Your father was deeply disturbed,' Seymour told her. 'He had naturally assumed Mr Parker, as a mill master, would have little sympathy with the vandals. But Mr Parker would persist in arguing against him and championing their cause. Indeed, for a moment I was quite concerned for Mr Brooke's health and well being.' He allowed his voice to trail away.

Caroline looked him directly in the face. 'Mr Seymour, this matter is very important to me and I want you to tell me the truth, however unpleasant. What exactly took place between my father and Mr Parker?'

Seymour put on a deeply serious expression. Whilst only too happy to paint Robert Parker in as black a shade as possible, he had no wish to give her any inkling of his scheming. 'He challenged Mr Brooke's views, he accused your father of being a liar, and . . . '

'Please continue,' she told him. 'I must know the full truth.'

'The truth is,' Seymour said quietly, 'that Mr Parker raised his hand to your father. Instead of leaving the house quietly when asked, he approached your father and threatened him. In fact the footmen had to be advised to restrain him if he took any further action.'

Caroline stared at Seymour in disbelief. She was aware of the killings and horror that went on in wars and in the lower classes. But violence at Brackenfield was unthinkable.

'Oh dear,' Seymour said regretfully, 'I'm afraid that I have upset you.'

'No, I'm grateful for your honesty. I'm beginning to see that I've a great deal to learn about the harsh realities of life.' Caroline gazed into some far distance, her face sad and lost.

Mr Seymour was just about to add a few more details when there was a further clatter of hooves outside. Both he and Caroline turned to look out of the window. A bay horse was cantering towards the house.

'Good heavens!' exclaimed Seymour as the rider handed the reins to a stable boy and strode up to the front door. 'Speak of the devil. It's Parker!'

Caroline stood up. A tremor of feeling went through her.

'Would you like me to instruct your man, Laidlaw, to tell him you're not able to receive any more visitors?' Seymour enquired. 'I think it would be wise to do so.'

Caroline wavered for a moment. 'I'm quite well enough, thank you,' she assured him, grateful for his concern, but not wishing to be dictated to.

'Then I will take my leave,' Seymour said tactfully, leaving her to deal with the agitation she felt at what she had just heard from Mr Seymour and what she should say to Mr Parker.

When he came in he made a brief, formal bow, then stood awkwardly in front of her, silent and unsmiling. She looked steadily back at him, and offered a curt nod.

'Please sit down, Mr Parker,' she told him, struggling to control her negative feelings.

He perched on the edge of a chair, ill at ease and still seeming uncertain how to begin. The impasse was broken unexpectedly by Caroline's little dog who suddenly showed an interest in the newcomer and ran up to him, putting his paws onto Robert's lap.

'No, Freddie, get down!' Caroline commanded. 'You mustn't jump up.'

'Please don't be cross with him,' Robert said, stroking the dog's head. 'I used to keep a dog myself when I was a child.' He looked up, and gave a brief smile.

Despite her reservations, Caroline was disarmed. She noticed that Robert

Parker had exceptionally fine brown eyes, so dark they were almost black. They were expressive eyes, full of feeling, and when he smiled his lips revealed faultless and beautiful teeth.

'I simply came to tell you how shocked I was to hear about your father's death,' Robert said abruptly.

He said the words with such raw, genuine feeling that Caroline felt her eyes suddenly fill with tears. 'Yes, it has been a shock for all of us,' she murmured. Now it was she who did not know what to say next. She fell silent, her grief once more overwhelming her.

Robert cleared his throat. 'I think you'll be aware, Miss Brooke, that Mr Brooke and I had a dispute on the night of his death.'

'Yes,' she responded swiftly, hopeful that Robert Parker might be able to provide some satisfactory explanation for his behaviour, and soothe the painful speculations which had been torturing her when she thought of her father's last hours of life.

He bowed his head. The silence lengthened.

'I gather that you were rather persistent in challenging my father's views,' Caroline said.

'Yes, that is true.'

Caroline looked at him perplexed. His face was hard and set, giving little away. He was clearly still jagged and uneasy, but was he feeling remorse or guilt? It was hard to tell.

'After the guests had left that night, my father was unusually troubled and upset,' she told him shortly. 'In fact he was so agitated that he refused to talk to me about what had happened.'

'I'm sorry to hear that,' Robert said.

'You're sorry!' Caroline exclaimed. 'Well, that's something in your favour, I'll admit, but isn't it a little late to talk about being sorry now? Shouldn't you have thought of my father's feelings when you started the dispute, long before it got out of hand?'

Robert looked at her, his expression wounded yet defiantly determined.

She waited for a moment. 'All he wanted from you was a simple apology. Surely that was not too much to ask. My father was an elderly and very respected man. Don't you agree that his opinions should have been deferred to?' Again she waited, but her visitor simply stared ahead of him, stern and unbending.

She could not see how Robert Parker could possibly now avoid offering his regrets and agreeing that he had been in the wrong. But he didn't. He continued to stroke the dog, his head bent. For Caroline his silence was an affront. She felt that he was the most unforthcoming, most stubborn man she had ever come across.

He looked up, meeting her gaze. 'I hope I showed your father the respect due to him, ma'am,' he told her. 'But I found it hard to apologise when I didn't believe myself to be in the wrong.'

Although he spoke very quietly, his voice steady and respectful, Caroline felt rage flare inside her. How dare he say those words? How dare he? She turned away, furious at his presumption, having no idea that Robert was torn apart with the desire to make amends and to comfort her.

'Miss Brooke,' he began, but she had turned away. When the door opened and she saw her Aunt Hilda beckoning her into the hall she went out immediately, leaving Robert sitting on his own, his heart pumping painfully after the disastrous conversation which had just taken place.

Beyond in the hall Aunt Hilda was flushed and concerned. 'Caroline, dear!' she whispered. 'You really should not be receiving visits from gentlemen on your own. Laidlaw tells me Mr Seymour has been visiting, and now Mr Parker is here.'

'Yes. They have come to offer their condolences, not to indulge in flirtations,' Caroline responded sharply. 'I am quite capable of speaking to them on my own.'

'It is not a question of being capable,

my dear. It is a matter of propriety. You should have sent for me to sit with you.'

'You were having your afternoon rest,' Caroline pointed out.

'You should have woken me, dear.'

'I am now mistress of this house, as you keep reminding me,' Caroline told her. 'I do not require a companion or a chaperone, and I shall receive whom I like in my own drawing room.'

Aunt Hilda stared at her in dismay. 'Yes, dear, very well,' she said in soothing tones. 'We won't argue about this now. I can see that you are on edge at the moment and feeling out of sorts.'

Caroline turned to go back into the drawing room. 'Aunt Hilda, please come and join us,' she said in a clear, ringing voice for her visitor's benefit. 'Mr Parker will not be staying long.'

Aunt Hilda had no wish to be unwelcoming and followed Caroline as instructed. She knew very little about Robert Parker's confrontation with her brother, simply that there had been some problem and that Arthur had had his nose put out of joint. She had always considered her brother to have a tendency to be overbearing, and was not inclined to be too severe in her judgement of Robert Parker.

'Mr Parker!' she said, holding out her hand to him as he rose to his feet.

He bowed. 'Good afternoon, Mrs Forsett. I came to express my sympathy for Miss Brooke's loss. And yours too, ma'am. But I think I've taken up enough of Miss Brooke's time. I should be leaving.'

'Your concern is appreciated, and you may be interested to know that Mr Brooke's funeral is to be held tomorrow,' Aunt Hilda told him, unable to resist giving out information. 'At two o'clock in our village church.'

Caroline looked at her aunt in horror. She was as good as inviting Mr Parker to attend her father's funeral when he was the last person who should be there.

'Thank you for that notification, ma'am,' Robert said politely.

'Of course,' Aunt Hilda continued, 'Caroline and I will not be attending. Ladies of our standing in society should never go to funerals.'

'Oh, how I wish I could go!' Caroline burst out impetuously. 'It is terrible to think that I shall not be there to say goodbye to my father when he goes to his last resting place.'

She glanced at Robert, her eyes flaring with emotion as she spoke.

'It is only poor women who go, because they have no shame about being seen overwhelmed by grief in public,' Aunt Hilda said firmly. 'And you have to remember, Caroline dear, that your father would have been shocked to think of his daughter flouting convention.'

'Yes, he would.' Caroline agreed. 'That is why I am going to abide by the convention, even though my heart goes against it.' She suddenly looked exhausted and sank down into a chair whereupon Freddie instantly ran to her and leapt up onto her knee, pawing her and licking her face. She gave a sad smile and hugged him against her, lost in thought.

Robert knew that it was now high time to leave, although as he walked out of the house he felt as though weights had been tied to his limbs. There had been so much left unsaid.

On the ride back to the mill he could feel Caroline Brooke's pain as though it was his own. Surrounded in material luxury, with only her affectionate but chivvying aunt for company, she seemed utterly bereft and abandoned. There seemed no person or creature in her life to love her simply for herself, with no concern for her status or her fortune. Except perhaps her dog.

He lay awake in the night, going over the rights and wrongs of attending Arthur Brooke's funeral. He recalled Edward Seymour's words as they passed each other in the hallway at Brackenfield. 'I am surprised you dare show your face here, sir.'

In the morning he decided he would

not go. He was not wanted; he had not been invited. But just before lunch he changed his mind again. He did not go so far as to enter the church, but waited respectfully outside, then followed the funeral party to the grave, standing a little distance away. He noted that Hugh Derby was amongst the mourners. And Edward Seymour also.

3

On the day following the funeral Caroline was visited by Mr Hattersley, who had been her father's attorney for many years. He was an old man now, wrinkled and bent.

'Dear Madam, I have come to inform you of the contents of your father's will,' he told her, settling himself behind the desk in Mr Brooke's study.

Caroline sat in quiet misery.

'I have to inform you, Miss Brooke that you are the main beneficiary of your father's will. He has left you the entire estate of Brackenfield; the house, its contents and all the land. In addition the asset and profits of Brackenfield Mill. And all his investments.' He paused. 'The bequest in its entirety represents a very considerable sum,' he said, his tone heavy and reflective.

'There's a bequest to Mr Brooke's

sister,' Mr Hattersley continued, 'and a small legacy for Mr Laidlaw, your father's butler. Also a legacy to Mr Cartwright, the current manager of Brackenfield Mill.'

He paused and coughed. 'And finally, Miss Brooke, I have to tell you of the provisos your father made regarding the way in which the money would pass to you.' He looked down at his papers and began to read in a flat, monotonous voice.

' 'In conclusion I, Arthur Henry Brooke, do give the remainder of my property, after all taxes, duties and costs have been paid, to my beloved daughter, Caroline, to be held in trust for her until she shall marry or until she shall have attained the age of thirty-five, whichever is the sooner.' '

Mr Hattersley glanced up and peered at her.

Caroline felt her heart give a painful beat. 'Please proceed.'

' 'All matters pertaining to the daily management and working of Bracken-field Mill, will be the responsibility of the aforementioned Mr Frederic Cartwright. As regards all matters pertaining to the administration, finances, or possible sale of the enterprise, these will rest with Mr William Derby, manufacturer in the town of Bradford in Yorkshire.

''Such decisions as need to be made for the continuance or closure of Brackenfield Mill are to be his sole responsibility during such time that my daughter, Caroline, remains unmarried and has not attained the age specified above.''

'Oh, heavens, what does this mean?' Caroline broke in. 'Is the mill to be sold? And Mr Derby to be the one who decides?'

'No, no, my dear. Your father simply wanted to include contingency clauses, in the event of there being any difficulties in the continued working of the mill.'

'But my father told me that the profits from the mill have been steadily rising in the past years.'

'Yes, but even the most secure businesses can run into difficulties,' Mr Hattersley ventured.

'So, Mr Derby is to be the sole decision-maker of what is best for Brackenfield Mill's future?' Caroline said softly.

'I am sure Mr Derby would inform you of any action he thought necessary regarding the mill.'

'But he could go ahead and do what he liked whatever my opinion.'

Mr Hattersley sighed. 'Miss Brooke, is it not usual for ladies to engage in complex business decisions, nor in transactions involving large amounts of money.'

'No.' Caroline found her hands were shaking. Why had her father done this? Given her everything, and then denied her access to it? And handed over the control of the mill to Mr Derby, a man she had always been wary of. 'Does this mean I shall have no business or money to support me until I marry or become an old maid?' she asked, feeling a stab of panic.

'No, no, my dear. You will be able to live most comfortably on the interest which will accrue from your father's investments. And Mr Derby has been entrusted to place a proportion of the profits from the mill into your bank account each year. The rest he will invest on your behalf.'

'So Mr Derby is to run the mill and also speculate with my money.' Caroline was in despair.

'My dear lady,' Mr Hattersley said, 'did you imagine you could administer this large fortune yourself? What do you know about the management of money? Or of making wise investments? And when did you last visit the mill, Miss Brooke?'

Caroline flushed. It was years since she had visited the mill. And her father only used to visit once a week to speak to his manager. Mr Cartwright had looked after all the mill's concerns.

'Dear Miss Brooke,' the attorney said

kindly, 'May I take the liberty of speaking frankly? All your worries could be resolved by making a judicious alliance. You could marry ma'am — '

'And then my husband would own the house and the mill,' Caroline flashed at him.

'Yes, of course. You would give these assets to him readily; man and wife being of one flesh. Think, my dear, a husband would be able to advise you — and have only your interests at heart.'

'Would he? Not necessarily, at least that is not what my Aunt Hilda tells me. Beware of fortune hunters is her advice.'

'And of course she is right. But not all men are fortune hunters.' Mr Hattersley gave a worldly chuckle. 'Those with a handsome fortune of their own are the best ones to look out for.'

Caroline realised that it was a waste of time continuing the discussion. She rose and thanked Mr Hattersley courteously for his advice. Having watched him climb into his chaise she went to find her aunt.

'My dear, you look so pale!' Aunt Hilda exclaimed. 'Have there been some upsets?'

'No, no. Papa has left matters very much as we would have expected.'

'Oh, thank the Lord for that!' her aunt exclaimed. 'One can never rest entirely easy until the contents of a will are laid out on the table.'

'And you, dear Aunt Hilda, are a few thousand pounds richer,' Caroline told her, smiling.

'Really. How agreeable. Do you know, I think I shall order a fine new dinner service that I've had my eye on for a while. So what have you planned for this afternoon, dear?' Aunt Hilda wondered.

'I thought I would make a visit to the mill,' Caroline said.

'The mill?' echoed her aunt, as though she had never heard of the place.

The first problem Caroline encountered in visiting Brackenfield Mill was finding out how to get inside it. Having instructed her coachman to wait for her in the mill yard, she walked up to the huge mill building, automatically expecting a servant to throw open the great closed doors and let her in, which was what happened whenever she paid visits elsewhere.

Realising the foolishness of this expectation, she walked around the side of the mill, looking up at the rows of windows running along its four storeys. It was an immense, sooty, unwelcoming place. She could hear the rhythmic clanking of machinery inside the building.

Beneath the clatters and bangs was a continual deep groaning roar she could not readily identify. Looking round she saw a small half open door set into the far end of the long wall.

The moment she stepped inside the building the noise became deafening. A man came walking towards her. 'Well now, what can I do for you, miss?' he asked, his eager glance skimming her from head to foot and back again with undisguised admiration.

Caroline found herself shocked at his direct, bold manner. 'I would like to speak with Mr Cartwright,' she said stiffly.

The man grinned suggestively. 'Would you indeed, miss?'

'Could you find him and tell him that Miss Caroline Brooke, the daughter of the late Mr Arthur Brooke, is here to see him.'

The man's expression instantly changed to one of anxious deference. 'Certainly, Miss Brooke.' He hurried down the corridor and knocked on the door. A tall, gaunt man emerged.

'Good afternoon, Mr Cartwright,' Caroline said, brushing away a black smut from her cheek.

'Please accept my regrets at Mr Brooke's death,' the manager said. 'If we had been expecting you, Miss Brooke, I could have made arrangements to have you met and properly welcomed on your arrival.' He looked decidedly aggrieved.

Caroline could not think what to do or say next, realising that there had been little purpose in coming to the mill other than to pay a visit and soothe her agitation about what Mr Hattersley had told her. But she had not identified any goal to achieve.

Paying and receiving visits formed a large part of her everyday life. And the main reason for these visits was simply to pass the time pleasantly in sociable conversation. In her social circle visiting was a means of entertainment and a purpose in itself.

Looking at Cartwright's stern, care-worn face whilst bracing herself against the relentless clamour battering her ears, she realised that the life of the mill was utterly different. The mill was a place of toil and production. If no work was done nothing was produced, no money was made. Her life of careless idleness took place in another world, as far from this world of noise and soot and labour as though thousands of miles separated them.

'I wondered if there were any possessions of my father's that I should collect and take back to Brackenfield,' she said in a sudden flash of inspiration.

Cartwright hesitated for a moment. 'Yes, Miss Brooke. His room is in some disorder, ma'am,' he said. 'If you would care to call again in another day or so, I would make sure everything was tidied and ready for you to look at.'

'I would like to look today,' Caroline told him, determined not to be fobbed off with lame excuses. 'Now, if you please.'

He nodded. 'Very well, ma'am. It is quite a way to walk,' he warned.

He led her up some steep stairs into the main part of the mill. The noise intensified as they approached one of the large working areas. Peering through the doors Caroline could see rows of tables piled with woollen fleeces. Men were standing beside them, their faces creased with concentration as they worked to untangle the strands.

'That's the combing room, ma'am,'

Cartwright told her, noting her interest. He had to shout to make himself heard. 'And farther on there is the main weaving shed.'

'Do you have the new power machines?' Caroline shouted back, her ears buzzing.

He nodded. 'Do you wish to see them, ma'am?'

As she followed him she felt her ears would explode, the assault on them was so severe. The room was filled with a double line of looms, all clattering away as the wooden struts on which the yarns were stretched moved backwards and forwards. She looked at the men supervising the looms and wondered how they could survive in this din and seeming chaos.

Cartwright went to stand beside one of the loom operators and gestured to Caroline to watch the moving shuttle. The machine was threaded with lines of yarn running from side to side and top to bottom. The shuttle threaded its way through the mesh with the swiftness of a bird on the wing. If it deflected a fraction from its determined path the operator would set it back on course.

Caroline was a quick and perceptive woman and instantly realised that the operator's task required great skill and deftness. Courage, too. A machine such as the one she was watching seemed as powerful and frightening as a danger-ous wild animal. It must be watched constantly.

This is a terrible, terrible place Caroline thought in horror. But she knew that the work must go on, so that profits were made. And people needed to work to feed their families. Her father had often told her so.

When they reached her father's office, Cartwright took a large bunch of keys from his pocket and unlocked the door. The room was dark, furnished solely with a large mahogany desk and chairs. Looking around Caroline could just make out a stack of papers, books and other small items, heaped together in a corner. She presumed this was the disorder Cartwright had referred to.

'Would you fetch candles?' she asked Cartwright, who was hovering behind her.

'When he had gone away, she made a rapid inspection of the items stacked on the floor, having a strange suspicion that there was something among them which Cartwright had not wanted her to see. She found little except bundles of charts relating to the mill's yearly progress. There were some handkerchief-sized samples of finished cloth scattered amongst empty cigar boxes and part burned tapers.

At the bottom of the heap was a carved wooden box with a tiny keyhole. Caroline was just about to examine it more closely when Cartwright returned.

'Have you found anything you care to take with you, Miss Brooke?' he asked.

Caroline returned to the little heap in the corner. 'I think I should like to take the little box,' she said on impulse, determined to have something to show from this depressing visit.

'Mr Brooke did not want the box disturbed, ma'am,' Cartwright said, with a note of warning. 'He gave orders for it to be disposed of.'

'Disposed of!' she exclaimed astonished. 'When did he order that?'

There was a short silence. 'Some years ago, ma'am. In the event of his death.'

'Are you absolutely sure about this?'

'Yes, ma'am. I had meant to carry out his orders later this afternoon. I have always taken a pride in serving your father promptly and in exact accordance with his wishes.'

Cartwright frowned and Caroline could tell that her unexpected arrival had been a blow to his pride.

'Surely this box should not be jettisoned,' she protested, bending to lift the box and examine it more closely. 'It is beautifully carved. And probably quite old.'

'I was planning to take it to the furnace this afternoon, Cartwright said stubbornly.

'You were going to burn it!' Caroline exclaimed, astonished. 'I won't allow that.'

Cartwright flinched. 'I can't believe you would feel comfortable to go against your father's express wishes, ma'am.'

'I think that is something only I can decide on,' she said, keeping her voice low, but firm.

'Yes, ma'am. Very well.' The manager's face was as blank as a stone.

'Is there a key?' she asked.

Cartwright shook his head.

Caroline frowned. 'Are you sure?'

'I've never seen one, ma'am.'

There was no more to say, and Caroline allowed Cartwright to escort her through the clamour of the mill and hand her into the waiting carriage. As the horses trotted through the gates she stared at the intriguing box on her lap feeling the dark thrill of a mystery to solve.

★   ★   ★

71

Robert planned the delivery of his new machines with the precision of a general preparing for a military expedition. The machine frames were being dispatched from a large foundry in the southern region of Yorkshire. They would be loaded on to two wagons each drawn by two dray horses.

The journey would take them over the steep wild moorland terrain separating south and west Yorkshire. Robert knew only too well the dangers of sabotage whilst the frames were in transit. He identified the two routes most suitable for loaded wagons. The plan then was for his foreman to set off whispers about the mill that one particular route was to be used, whilst in reality the other route would be taken.

'It's a fair shame that we've got to be suspecting men as work alongside us o' being wreckers,' the foreman commented grimly.

'Indeed it is,' Robert agreed. 'But they are the ones who will be most affected by the installation of the machines. There would well be men in our mill eagerly waiting for information to pass to powerful organisations who are making a business out of treachery and destruction.'

'There are some as say that high up folks are in wi' the ruffians making trouble,' the foreman observed. 'It's hard to credit, ain't it?'

'It could well be true,' Robert observed.

'But why would they do it? Rich folks as want for nothing?'

'Rich folks sometimes want for occupation and excitement,' Robert said. 'Let's pray they don't get any excitement out of our machines.' Because if they do, he thought, I truly will be ruined.

Caroline, meanwhile, was trying to find a key to open the mysterious oak box she had brought back from Brackenfield Mill. Feeling furtive and guilty she slid into her father's bedroom and looked cautiously around her, her eyes instantly drawn to the place on the floor where her father had fallen and lain dead.

On the dresser, neatly laid out, were some of the personal possessions her father used to keep about his person. There were a few coins, a silver and enamel case containing his snuff, a gold watch and a clean, unused handkerchief. But no keys. She frowned in concentration. Where would I keep such a key, she asked herself. She pondered for a few moments. Of course! She would keep it about her person, in a pocket, or pinned inside the neckline of a gown.

She opened her father's wardrobe and looked for the coat he had been wearing on the night of the dinner party. Gently, she slipped her fingers into the outer pockets of his coat. They were empty. But feeling inside one of the slender openings in the lining of the coat she felt something cold and smooth. Pulling it free she found a tiny brass key on a delicate link chain.

Returning to her room she had the box opened in seconds. But apart from a lock of sable hair, it was completely empty.

★ ★ ★

Robert stood at the window, his ears straining for the sounds of rumbling wheels. The wagons bringing the replacement machines had been expected around six. And now it was near eight.

He stood at a window looking out. There was just darkness across the distant moor. The night was black and the air stagnant and still, as though it were holding its breath. He prayed that the machines and the men he had sent to escort them were safe.

He went down to the furnace room where the new boiler was installed. The coal was stacked in the furnace, waiting to be lit. The water in the boiler would heat and bubble and the trapped steam would build pressure in the pipes; a fearsome, roaring power to drive his machines. A spark of excitement flared within him at the prospect. He visualised the cloth being created in the twinkling of an eye, his warehouse filling with stock to sell.

He stiffened, hearing the heavy clatter of the hooves of great dray horses. They were here. He ran out into the yard. The horses had come to a halt. Steam rose from them, a white pillow of vapour in the cold air.

'Now, then sir,' his foreman called out, coming forward to greet him. 'We are all back safe and sound. Machines, men and horses!'

The drivers got down from the wagons and there was a warm shaking of hands all round.

'Come inside!' Robert told them. 'There are meat pies and plenty of hot punch. I've left the curtains pulled back so we can see any would-be intruders.'

Let them dare come, Robert thought, watching his hired hands wolfing down their suppers. Evil influences would surely slink away shamefaced in the face of the simple jubilation of these brave, loyal men.

Less than two days later the machines were installed and in operation and Robert was filled with a rush of new optimism, a sense that his luck was about to change.

★ ★ ★

On the Sunday at the end of that week he decided he would go to church to offer up thanks for the granting of his recent prayers. In choosing to attend the village church of Brackenfield he knew that he was secretly hoping to see Caroline Brooke once more and perhaps gain an opportunity to speak to her.

Rumours were now rife that Miss Caroline Brooke was a rich heiress. Robert judged she was in a highly vulnerable situation. He wondered what provision her father might have made to protect her from rogues and liars and those motivated only by greed.

He had no thoughts of winning her

for himself. What rich, beautiful, well-to-do young woman such as Caroline would even consider him? A bluff self-made businessman, who had not yet fully established himself.

Walking into the church he sat in an empty pew. He saw her two rows in front, her Aunt Hilda beside her. Her hair, gathered into a knot at the nape of her neck beneath her bonnet, gleamed in the light from the altar candles.

He could not pull his gaze away from her. Slowly the realisation that something momentous was happening to him began to dawn.

At the end of the service he watched the congregation file out, wondering how he could contrive an opportunity to speak to her.

She walked down the aisle, looking straight ahead of her, remote and dignified. Mrs Forsett came along behind.

Outside the church the congregation loitered in small groups. Robert watched Caroline exchange a few words with a number of people who made a point of seeking her out.

He also noticed Seymour, chatting agreeably and making himself known. Eventually a moment came when Mrs Forsett's attention was diverted and Caroline was left temporarily on her own.

Robert walked forward. 'Miss Brooke,' he said softly as he stood in front of her.

She turned to look at him. 'Mr Parker,' she responded with cold politeness.

'I hope you are well ma'am,' he said, cursing himself for his lack of ingenuity.

'Quite well, thank you.'

Robert saw the heavy shadows under her eyes and understood how much she had been suffering since her father's death. And yet she stood facing him, brave and proud.

'Miss Brooke, I simply wanted to say that I hope you do not still think badly of me.'

There was a short silence. 'Mr Parker,' she responded, 'you need not trouble yourself on that account. I do not think of you very much at all.'

He stared back in dismay.

'I am sorry if I seem unkind, sir,' she said formally. 'I did not mean to be impolite, but your coming to speak to me like this offends me.'

'Offends you! I am very sorry to hear that.'

'Perhaps I should explain myself. I think that in view of what happened on the night of my father's death, you should be well advised to leave me in peace,' she said icily. She glanced around her. 'Ah, there is my aunt looking for me. Good day, Mr Parker.'

That was all. She was gone. He felt like a boy, chided for some misdemeanour and then dismissed. He watched her walk away and blend herself into the little group around her aunt. He then watched as Seymour joined the group, placing himself beside Caroline and smiling down at her.

Robert found himself clenching his hands tight with envy at the other man's social deftness, and at the way in which Caroline glanced up at him, her face suddenly illuminated with a smile.

Robert was perfectly aware of what was happening to him. He had been in love before as a young man. It had not been a happy experience. The lady in question had been several years older than Robert. She had flattered him, teased and flirted with him.

He had believed every word she had huskily whispered into his ear. And then, one day, quite casually, she had told him that she had become engaged to a rich widower.

Robert had decided that happiness lay in work not in love. At the age of twenty-one, he had decided to rent an old cloth mill which he found in an out-of-the-way district on the outskirts of the town. It was damp and dilapidated and full of creaky old machinery. But there were plenty of willing workhands as the cottage industries were slowly dying and the unemployed spinners and weavers considered any work was better than none.

In two years he had made enough profit to put down a deposit on a newer mill, situated close to the highroad on the River Aire.

Riding away from the church that winter morning, he remembered the day he took possession of the keys to the new mill to which he had already given his name. He remembered pushing open the great wooden doors and walking through every room of the silent, empty building. Parker Mill. A thrill of anticipation had rushed through him like a gale.

His thoughts veered back to Caroline Brooke. He knew that she had had the spoiled upbringing of a rich young woman. And that she was dignified and proud. But he did not think it was a pride based on cold vanity. Rather a determination not to be ground down by sorrow and the vulnerability of her sex. It hurt him to think of her loneliness and her struggles as a helpless woman in a harsh world.

He sighed. He had no illusions as to her hold over him. She pulled him like a magnet. And there was nothing he could do about it. He could almost hear fate mocking him with cruel laughter.

He pressed his heels against the flanks of his horse. Sensing his mood the animal broke into a gallop and took him speedily back to his mill.

On the way home from church Aunt Hilda told Caroline that she felt it was time she went back to her own house to discover what the servants had been up to in her absence. 'Of course, I wouldn't dream of going if you were not feeling well enough to be on your own,' she said.

'Of course you must go, Aunt Hilda. I shall be perfectly able to manage.' Caroline told her.

'Naturally if you wished to receive a gentleman, for example Mr Seymour, I should be available at any time to come along and act as chaperone.'

'Mr Seymour had only visited twice,'

Caroline reminded her.

'Hmm. I watched him when you were speaking together after church. He is always most attentive. And, you, my dear, have given every indication of enjoying his company.'

'Yes, he always has something amusing to say, I must admit.'

'I've been thinking,' said her aunt, with a gleam of calculation, 'that if I returned home I could arrange one or two little luncheon parties to cheer you up. Very quiet affairs, naturally, as we are still in mourning. But I do think it's a shame for you to be shut up here in Brackenfield like a nun.'

'That is kind,' Caroline said, sighing internally, and reflecting that her aunt's intention was to dangle her in front of possible husbands as though she were a juicy bone to tempt a dog.

4

The output of cloth at Robert's mill increased dramatically once the new steam-powered looms were fully operative. He was able to fulfil all his prior commitments for the delivery of cloth, and had no hesitation in giving promises on two further large orders which had recently come in.

Returning to his house one March afternoon for a late bite of lunch he found a printed card amongst the mail. It was from Mrs John Forsett of Fir Tree Lodge, inviting him to join her and a few friends for a luncheon party on the following Sunday. Mrs Forsett had scribbled a postscript, letting Robert know that this would be a small quiet affair, bearing in mind the recent death of her brother, Mr Arthur Brooke.

Robert was astonished. He had

realised that Mrs Forsett was one of those slightly eccentric people who preached the gospel of convention, but was quite happy to wave it aside when it suited her. Giving a luncheon party so soon after her brother's death was decidedly irregular. But to invite a virtual stranger — and an unattached bachelor into the bargain - to come as a guest on his own was downright peculiar.

Especially when the man was out of favour with her niece, his name blackened in her eyes. But perhaps Mrs Forsett knew nothing about the unpleasant confrontation in Mr Brooke's dining-room. Maybe Caroline had kept her misgivings to herself.

His heart began to race as he considered the prospect of meeting Caroline Brooke once more. It was perfectly obvious that she would be a guest at the luncheon too. And it seemed equally obvious, albeit astounding, that Mrs Forsett must have some thoughts of him as a possible suitor. He wondered how many other likely beaux had been invited. Poor, bereft Caroline — to be paraded before the bachelors of Yorkshire like a dumb creature brought to market.

Caroline kept returning to her father's mahogany box and the lock of hair inside it. It was certainly not her mother's, whose hair had been light brown. She stared at it, strangely troubled.

One morning, while guiding her pony, Opal, along the boundaries of the Brackenfield Estate, she saw Edward Seymour riding on the other side of the stone wall.

'Good-day, Miss Brooke!' he called out, sweeping off his hat. 'I hope you are well.'

'And you too, sir.'

'Most certainly. Aside from being quizzed mercilessly on my views of marriage and being paired off with every marriageable lady in the district.'

'Should I be sorry for you?' Caroline asked.

'Indeed you should, Miss Brooke. Listen to whom they have chosen for me; Miss Derby with her long red nose, and a whole tribe of others, whose names I've quite forgotten.'

'Mr Seymour! Shame on you!' Caroline reproved him, but she could not help smiling.

'Do you think I should make an offer to one of those ladies, Miss Brooke? Or not?'

Caroline caught her breath at his flirtatious boldness. 'I wouldn't presume to advise you on such an important matter, Mr Seymour,' she said formally.

'I should not have asked the question,' he returned swiftly. 'Please forgive me.'

They rode on in silence for a few moments. 'So, Miss Brooke, did you ride out this morning to look over your estate and ensure that all was well?' Seymour enquired with reassuring impartiality.

'I simply thought it was a fine

morning and it would be pleasant to take a ride.'

'Mmm. Do you have a good gamekeeper you can trust?' he asked.

'Yes, indeed. Ned Sherringham. He lives in a cottage on the east boundary of the estate.'

'And no doubt you will be arranging regular meetings with Sherringham so that you can give him instruction and keep an eye on his work,' Seymour suggested.

Caroline felt a prick of alarm. 'Oh, my father always trusted him entirely. And so do I.'

'Ah, but Sherringham must learn to account to his new mistress. If you don't keep your servants on their toes, they will soon rest on their laurels.' Seymour raised an eyebrow.

'My father has only recently died,' Caroline protested. 'I have not yet been able to see to all the affairs which need my attention.' Waves of guilt, inadequacy and panic-stricken helplessness rolled through her as she considered all that was to be done.

'But of course,' Seymour said sooth-ingly. 'Perhaps you would like me to speak to Sherringham. 'I've learned a great deal about gamekeepers and estate managers since I took over Kelshaw Hall.'

Caroline was torn. She longed for advice and support. But she did not want to be thought empty-headed and weak. Moreover, who was she to trust, really trust?

'Thank you, I will certainly think the matter over,' responded Caroline politely, before bidding Seymour good-day and turning her pony back towards the house.

Seymour observed her departure. He recalled the deep blue of her eyes, the sincerity of her expression, her erect figure in the black riding pelisse shown off to perfection on that showy cream and white pony.

If she had been moving in London society instead of barbarian Bradford, she would have been snapped up long ago. Moreover the notion of her huge wealth was enough to set any man's pulse racing with expectation. Seymour saw her as a ripe plum about to drop off the tree — if it were to be given just a little shake.

On arriving back at the house, Caroline went straight up to her room. The meeting with Edward Seymour had left her unsettled. His company always had that effect. His charm drew her towards him, but his boldness made her cautious.

She was suddenly overtaken with a feeling of recklessness and devil-may-care. She seized the oak box, threw open the lid and vowed she would finally discover if it had any secrets to tell. Taking up her sewing scissors she began to make little stabs against the lining.

Despite her guilt at damaging the box, her stabs became more urgent until eventually there was the sound of a spring snapping, and the base of the box suddenly lifted. Beneath were some folded papers. A shiver ran through her as she unfolded the first sheet.

It was dated 14 June 1791

My most precious girl,

Since we talked yesterday I have not been able to eat or sleep. My dear one, the news you gave me was like a miracle. There are no words to express my happiness and gratitude.

I know you feel great anxiety about the situation you find yourself in. but I shall never abandon you. And you most certainly will never need to be worn down by the cares of poverty for the rest of your life.

We will meet again tomorrow at the same place and talk over what must be done.

I love you now and always and am ever your most devoted and faithful protector.

A

Caroline's heart beat painfully as she stared down at the lines on the page. Who was this *precious girl*? A poor relative, perhaps. She tried to think of reasons to convince herself that what her father had written was based on good and kindliness, but all the time a disobedient inner voice was protesting. Betrayal, Infidelity, Intrigue. She spread out the second sheet.

16 June 1791

My sweet girl,

I know that you were shocked by my proposal when we spoke yesterday. But it is of no use to cry over spilt milk. When troubles come we must do whatever is practical and possible. We must look ahead to the future and remember our duties and obligations to our loved ones.

Dearest one, I beg you to promise that you will at least think about my proposal. It is the only choice we have. Be brave, my love. All will be well.

I am, as you must surely believe now, your devoted champion and defender.

A

P.S. Guard this letter well. It must be seen only by your eyes and that other worthy person we can both trust.

Caroline dropped the paper as

though it were on fire. There was no doubt now about betrayal. Her father had been deceiving her mother, forming a passionate alliance with another woman. Here in these letters was the father she had known and loved. And another man altogether.

She read through the letters again. Her heart was thundering in her chest, but she forced herself to read each betraying word. Suddenly a new realisation came to her. This 'trouble' her father referred to could only mean one thing. The vile woman he had been consorting with was carrying his child. She gave an involuntary groan of revulsion.

So — who was this mysterious woman? And where was her baby? This unknown person who was Caroline's unknown half-brother or sister.

She looked at the sheets again, holding the paper up to the light to see if anything previously invisible might show through. On the last sheet she saw a faint shadow in one corner. Turning the sheet over she discovered some scribbles, so faint they were barely decipherable. She took the sheet to the window to gain more light. Eventually she was able to make something out. It looked like *E. Bell, 8 Alfred Terrace*.

The information slotted instantly into her memory, lodging tight there whether she liked it or not. She replaced the letters in the box, hid the box in the wardrobe, then rang for Susan.

'Please go and instruct the coachman to prepare the carriage,' she told her. 'I shall be driving into Bradford within the hour.'

'Yes, madam.' Susan hesitated. 'Would you like me to go with you, madam?' she asked with deference. 'It is . . . safe to go out into the town on your own?'

She means is it proper for a young woman to walk about in the town on her own, thought Caroline. And she is right to ask. But how can I take a companion on this mission?

'I shall be quite safe,' she told Susan

with calm authority.

It was starting to rain as Caroline's coachman manoeuvred the carriage through the tightly-packed network of streets in which Alfred Terrace was situated. The tiny houses seemed to be hunched together, bracing themselves against the rain and the wind.

Through an alleyway she glimpsed the walls of a soot-blackened mill. Smoke churned from its chimney, drifting upwards to blend the thick cloud of vapour which hung over the area like a great grey lid.

As they reached the end of Alfred Terrace she asked the coachman to wait, realising that it might be alarming for the inhabitants of number 8 to see a large gleaming four-in-hand drawing up. Walking along the cobbles, she held up her skirts to prevent their being soiled by the dirt and litter underfoot. As the rain fell to the ground it turned black with filth. Her shoes were soon soaked and stained.

Having located number 8, she stood

for a moment with her hand poised to tap on the door. Her heart began a frantic beating. The door was opened by a pale, thin woman huddled inside a thick knitted shawl. She looked Caroline up and down.

'I'm looking for a Miss or Mrs E Bell,' Caroline said, trying to sound politely neutral.

'You won't find her here, I'm afraid,' the woman said in a low flat voice.

'Do you know her?' Caroline's whole body trembled with feeling.

The woman nodded. Her face was guarded now, as though she were hiding secret thoughts.

'My name is Caroline Brooke. I was hoping I might be able to speak with Mrs Bell.'

The woman sighed. 'You'd best come in, Miss Brooke. You'll be getting soaked standing out there.' she stood aside and Caroline passed through the narrow doorway into a low, cramped room with a stone-flagged floor.

'Sit yourself down,' the woman said,

pointing to a small sofa beneath the room's only window which looked out on to the street.

She took lumps of coal from a bucket and threw them on to the small smouldering fire. Taking a long poker she prodded the new coals until a few flames began to flicker. She turned to look at Caroline. 'You've been having a sad time since Mr Brooke died,' she said.

'Oh!' Caroline was taken aback. 'You've heard about that?'

'Certainly, I've heard. He was a big man in this town, your father.' The woman straightened up, placing a hand on the small of her back and grimacing. Beneath her shawl she wore a roughly-woven, sand-coloured cotton frock and white apron. There was a thin, pinched look about both her face and her figure. But she had beautiful thick dark hair.

'Yes, I suppose so.' Caroline paused, wondering what to say next. 'Could you be kind enough to tell me where I might find Mrs Bell?' she asked tentatively.

'In heaven, I should hope,' the thin woman said, sinking into a chair. 'She's been dead these last twenty years.'

'No!' Caroline cried out, surprised that the knowledge should cause her such distress. 'Surely she was only very young when she died?'

'Twenty-one, just gone,' the woman confirmed. 'Same age as you are now, Miss Brooke.'

Caroline stared at her.

'I must be straight with you,' the woman said. 'I knew who you were the minute I saw you on the doorstep.'

'How could you know?' Caroline demanded.

'I've kept track on you since you were a little baby.' The woman's gaze was not flinty and direct. 'Tell me why you've come today, Miss Brooke, and then tell me what you know. And, after that, then we'll see what I can tell you extra.'

'I don't know if I can do that,' Caroline said, hesitating. 'I've found things out, it's true. But I don't think I can give secrets to a stranger.'

The woman gave a harsh, dry laugh. 'I'm not a stranger, miss. The Mrs E Bell you speak of was my sister, Eliza. And we had no secrets from each other. Never a one.'

Caroline stared at her in bewilderment. 'Eliza Bell was your sister!'

'Ay, she was. My only sister.' The woman was looking at her with sharp speculation. 'I see how it is. You've been digging about, and you've found his letters. Have I guessed right?'

Caroline nodded.

'The old devil! He promised me he'd burn them.'

Caroline sensed the power of feeling that was burning within this woman. In the face of it she herself felt helpless and redundant.

The woman turned slowly to face her. 'You may think I'm hard and cruel to speak like that of your father. But if you knew all that had happened, you'd know why I'm so angry.'

Caroline flinched. 'Yes,' she agreed helplessly, not understanding at all. 'I can appreciate that you must feel angry. It was wrong of me to intrude on you like this.'

'No! You did right to come. I don't know how you got hold of them letters, but you must have had a terrible shock when you read them.' There was a pause. 'How much do you know?' the woman demanded.

'That Eliza was his . . . That he and Eliza had an understanding,' Caroline finished miserably.

'That's one way of putting it,' the woman said, her face grim.

'I came to the conclusion that she . . . that Eliza was carrying his child.'

'Ay, well you were right.'

'I wanted to know about the baby Eliza was carrying,' Caroline ventured. 'Was it a boy or a girl?'

'A girl,' the woman said softly.

Caroline felt an internal jolt. 'So I have a half-sister. Is she still alive? Where can I find her?'

'You'll not need to look far.' The woman's lips were a tight thin line.

'Oh, my poor mama!' Caroline cried out, suddenly overwhelmed with feeling. 'Thank God she didn't have any idea about the terrible things which were going on whilst she carried me.'

The woman made a low noise in her throat. 'Miss Brooke, this will come as a dreadful shock to you. But the mother you're talking about was not what you thought.' She stopped. 'She was the one who cared for you and reared you. But it was another who gave you life.'

Caroline stared at her in disbelief. 'I beg your pardon.'

'There is no half-sister, Miss Brooke,' the woman said. 'The baby Eliza was carrying was you.'

Caroline closed her eyes. Her heart was making small explosions in her chest. 'You mean that Eliza Bell was my real mother?' The shock reverberated through her, more piercing and turbulent than anything she had ever known.

'Yes, Eliza, my little sister. She bore you in this house, and on the very same day your father took you away to

102

Brackenfield to be brought up as the daughter of himself and Mrs Brooke.'

The woman's face had now set hard and grim. 'I think you should go now, Miss Brooke. You've stirred up a right storm inside me. I can't see what use there can be in staying any longer. You just be content with being Miss Brooke of Brackenfield — mistress of a great house and a mill into the bargain. You're entitled to all he's left you. You're Mr Arthur Brooke's daughter and no-one can argue with that.' She pressed her lips together tightly. 'And besides, my husband'll be coming home soon.'

'Yes, I'll go,' said Caroline, her body shaking with shock. She turned back as her hand reached for the door knob. 'Will you tell me your name?' she whispered.

'Mary. Mary Bracegirdle.'

'Might I come and see you again?' Caroline asked humbly.

'You must do as you please. I can't stop you, can I?' Mary Bracegirdle's face registered the resignation of the poor when confronting the powerfulness of the rich. But she was proud, too.

Caroline could not find an adequate reply. 'Good day,' she said. 'And thank you for speaking to me.'

On arriving at Brackenfield, Laidlaw gave her a note that had been delivered in her absence. It was from Aunt Hilda. A bright, cheery reminder of her luncheon party on the coming Sunday, and how much she was looking forward to it.

She wondered what Aunt Hilda's reaction would be if she were to find out that her niece was not the lady of gentle birth everyone had always believed her to be. That she was the result of an illicit union between her father and a working girl. That Caroline Brooke of Brackenfield was the illegitimate child of a poor wretch who had no cultural refinements or education.

Caroline knew that no respectable man would want a wife with such a stain on her heritage. The gentlemen in her parents' circle of society, those she had been brought up with as an equal, would scorn a girl such as Eliza Bell. And she, Caroline, carried Eliza's blood in her veins. As yet it was a secret. But could she keep that secret? And if she ever learnt to love a man in the future, could she deceive him?

And, most frightening of all, didn't secrets have a way of being found out when one least expected it. How could she live under that cloud of fear? She was doomed to spinsterhood, to spend her life lonely and isolated from all she had been brought up to expect.

5

Aunt Hilda's household at Fir Tree Lodge was nothing on the scale of Brackenfield. But Hilda Forsett was comfortably wealthy and was determined that she would make as good an impression with her little luncheon party as any hostess living in a country manor house or elegant residence in London.

The first guests to arrive were Amelia Derby, her sister Emma, and her brother, William. After them came Edward Seymour, driving a sporting curricle drawn by two prancing chestnut horses, closely followed by Robert on his bay horse.

Aunt Hilda began to grow anxious. What had happened to delay Caroline? Had there been some mishap? Had her coach come to some harm? Her imagination began to run riot.

The time for serving lunch came and went. Then a black-robed rider on a cream pony appeared, moving at a slow steady pace down the drive, a little dog trotting in attendance. Aunt Hilda gave a little gasp. Caroline had come on horseback — and bringing her spaniel! What was she thinking of? And looking so dreadfully white and woebegone.

On entering the room, Caroline addressed the company with solemn dignity. 'I am very sorry to have kept you all waiting,' she said, making no attempt to offer an explanation.

Aunt Hilda tutted a little then led the guests in to lunch. At first the atmosphere was quiet and uncertain, but Edward Seymour came to the rescue, recounting stories about the local huntsmen, mimicking their north country accents and raising some laughter. Aunt Hilda then asked William Derby if he had plans to join his father in the management of Derby Mill.

William Derby stiffened. 'No, ma'am.

I have no plans in that direction whatsoever.'

Miss Derby elaborated for him. 'My father does not want William to have anything to do with the mill, Mrs Forsett. He feels that all his own efforts in promoting the success of the mill would be wasted if his son were to become a mere tradesman.' Her eyes slid to Robert, her glance tinged with disdain.

There was a short silence. Seymour gave his lazy smile. 'Maybe we should not be so swift to despise tradesmen, Miss Derby,' he remarked. 'We all of us have our allotted place in life. Although I must admit, I thank my lucky stars I was not born the sort of fellow who has to slave in order to buy his own house and furniture because there is nothing to inherit.'

'If there were no businessmen and traders to slave and create new wealth, sir,' Robert responded evenly, 'your estates would go to rack and ruin from lack of funds and you might even be obliged to sell your furniture and live on the streets.'

Robert calmly continued eating his lunch, unruffled by Seymour's barbs. What was troubling him far more was Caroline's pale, grief-stricken face. He longed to speak to her, to comfort her.

'I have only visited my father's mill once,' Miss Derby volunteered. 'It is a dreadful place. It smells of steam and oily machinery and people who are not washed. And the noise is perfectly deafening. I don't know how you can bear it, Mr Parker.'

'I have heard noise some people call music which is far more disagreeable,' Robert commented with a dry smile. 'Although I'm sure that wouldn't apply to the piano when you are playing it, Miss Derby.'

Miss Derby fell silent, not knowing whether to look pleased or offended.

Aunt Hilda was becoming more and more concerned about her niece who had hardly touched her food and not spoken a word. Poor, dear Caroline.

Something was terribly wrong.

It was five in the afternoon as the company began to disperse. Aunt Hilda waved as the Derbys and Edward Seymour drove off. Then Caroline's pony and Robert's horse were brought round from the stables.

Well aware that her aunt's eyes were on her, Caroline went unhesitatingly to stand beside Robert, who was bending down against his horse to check the tightness of the girth strap.

'Mr Parker,' she said in a low voice, claiming his attention.

He turned, surprised. His expressive dark eyes registered concern and sympathy. 'Miss Brooke?'

'I want to tell you that I'm sorry about the ill-mannered way I spoke to you outside the church some time ago,' she told him. 'It was wrong of me to say what I did. And it was unfair to give you no chance of making a reply.'

Robert was aware of the increased beating of his heart. Her frank humility touched him deeply. 'I believe I too have been in the wrong, Miss Brooke,' he told her.

'How so?' she asked steadily.

'There are matters concerning the night of your father's death that I should have explained to you more fully. But at first I was too proud. And afterwards I was faint-hearted. I think it is I who have a good deal to apologise for.'

He looked up at the sky which was sullen and grey. 'Miss Brooke,' he said, 'there is going to be rain and it will soon be growing dark. Perhaps you would permit me to ride with you and ensure that you return safely to Brackenfield. I shall go and tell Mrs Forsett, and put her mind at rest about your safety,' he said gravely. And for the first time that afternoon Caroline gave a genuine smile.

'It was kind of you to reassure Aunt Hilda,' Caroline informed him as they rode away. 'She has been like a mother to me since my own mother died.'

'Then it is good that she is nearby

and here to comfort you when you need her. You must have felt very alone since your father's death.' Robert was aware that his awkwardness and reserve with her had suddenly evaporated.

There was a pause. 'I've learned a great deal in the weeks since my father died,' she said. 'I've discovered that things I have always taken for granted are not nearly as safe and secure as I had thought. And that things and, indeed people, are not what they always seemed.'

She drew her pony's reins more tightly through her fingers. 'Mr Parker, I have been thinking about my father a great deal in the past weeks, trying to understand what might have disturbed him so much on the night he died. You told me that you had a dispute with him, yet I can't understand why my father should have been so angry. He often used to say how much he enjoyed a good 'battle of words'.'

'Yes, I can believe that.' Robert said thoughtfully.

'Mr Seymour told me that you called my father a liar,' Caroline said in a low voice. 'That you raised your hand to him,' Caroline said.

'Good God! Did he indeed. He must wish to paint the blackest picture of me,' Robert exclaimed.

'So, what Mr Seymour said is not true?'

'It is not a total lie. I challenged your father's remark that every worker had the potential to be a vandal and a machine wrecker. Your father became extremely angry. He claimed that I was calling him a liar. I think we were both at fault, and I just wish that I had found some way to appease him. Through my stubbornness your father was made agitated and upset. And only a few hours later he was dead. Do you think I haven't blamed myself?'

'No, I'm sure you have.'

'And what of the claim that you raised a hand to my father?'

Robert hesitated. He hated to tell her what had happened, her father losing his gentlemanly control, the ugly anger in his face. 'I had no intention of raising my hand to him to do him harm,' he said. 'The truth of the matter is that I . . . put my hands up in front of me — '

'To defend yourself,' she interposed quietly.

'Yes.'

'My father did have a fiery temper,' Caroline said sadly. 'Especially with the servants.'

Robert sighed. 'Your father was a remarkable and greatly-respected man, Miss Brooke. You can be proud of his memory.'

'Yes, yes, he was remarkable.' She glanced up at the low grey clouds, her face reflective and sorrowful. 'Are your parents still alive, Mr Parker?' she asked suddenly.

'They died within the last two years. I miss them both.'

'I'm truly sorry,' she said, and he was moved to hear the tenderness in her voice. Suddenly she turned and gave him a beautiful and wistful smile.

Robert felt a surge of joy and a thrill of anticipation. She had understood all that he had told her of the clash with her father.

As they rode together down the long drive to Brackenfield he was planning what he should say to her before they parted. Perhaps he could suggest that they take a ride in the park one afternoon. Or maybe he could arrange a reciprocal lunch at his house. Caroline would not feel compromised to visit him at home if Mrs Forsett were accompanying her. He could surely hope.

But when he next looked at her, he saw instantly that her manner had mysteriously reverted to her earlier restrained sadness. Once again she looked as stiff and unreachable as a statue.

As they reached the house a stable boy came running up to take Caroline's pony to his stall. The front door of the house opened and a grave-faced man-servant stepped forward to greet her.

Caroline gathered her little spaniel into her arms. 'Thank you for accompanying me home, Mr Parker. Good night.' She turned and walked into the house.

The next morning Caroline had a visit from her gamekeeper, Ned Sherringham, insisting that she should permit him to order and install a mantrap near the boundary walls of the estate in order to keep out the gypsies who had settled in the woods close by.

'They'll be coming over the wall at night and tekkin' our birds and rabbits. They're varmin, ma'am. The traps'd frighten 'em off.'

'But mantraps are terrible things!' Caroline protested.

'Your father was all for getting one,' Sherringham said.

'I need to think about this,' Caroline said uncertainly. 'I'll let you know what I decide.'

Sherringham left looking disgruntled and Caroline sank down on a chair, overwhelmed with cares and responsibilities. 'Oh, Father, if only you were still here!' she cried out impulsively. But voicing that plea only led to more turbulence. Although she still missed her father dreadfully, her thoughts about him were undergoing a troubling and painful change. How could the indulgent father she had loved all her life have behaved so cruelly to his wife and his mistress?

He had always expressed such high moral principles. And yet he had been a seducer, an adulterer and a deceiver. And what was she to make of Robert Parker's account of the dispute just before her father's death? Robert had been kind, trying to show her father in as good a light as he could manage, but Caroline was beginning to have doubts.

She knew she would have no respite from her inner turmoil until she had been told the whole story of what happened in those terrible months before her birth. Having sat brooding for a time with her head in her hands, she suddenly sprang up. Within the half-hour she was in the coach and on the way once again to Alfred Terrace.

It took great courage to walk down the narrow street and knock at the little door again.

Mary Bracegirdle's greeting was wary. 'Miss Brooke.'

Caroline felt tears well up.

'Oh, you poor thing!' Mary exclaimed. 'You look all used up. Come in!'

Caroline perched uneasily on the little sofa. The room was filled with steam from the washing Mary took in to earn some money for little treats.

'Don't look so full of woe,' Mary said. 'I don't harbour any grudge against you.' Her eyes swept over Caroline in a loving glance. 'Eliza's little baby,' she murmured.

Caroline sprang up and suddenly the two women had their arms round one another, sobbing and clinging together.

'Ahh, I've thought of you so often, over the years, wondering how you were growing up,' Mary said.

'Will you tell me about Eliza?' Caroline asked. 'What sort of person she was, and how it came about that my father . . . '

Mary put her arm around her niece. 'You would have been proud to have her as a mother. She was tall, and always held herself very straight. Her beauty made men turn and look at her. And she's passed that beauty on to you.'

'But what was she like — as a person?'

'She was full of life and adventure and curiosity. And there she was, poor lass, little more than a child, and penned up working in the mill with the noise and clatter from morning 'til night.

'But why did she have to work in the mill from such a young age?' Caroline exclaimed.

'By the time I was married, both our parents were dead. Eliza came to live with us, but we had no money to keep her.' Mary Bracegirdle gave a shrug of resignation.

Caroline found it incomprehensible

that people should be in such hardship and want. 'How did she meet my father?'

'When she was seventeen she went to work at Brackenfield Mill. I reckon your father took a fancy to her the first time he saw her. He started giving her little presents. A pretty silver bracelet, a silk shawl. And then he would slip her a half-crown every so often — it were a lot o' money for folks like us.'

Mary pressed her lips together. 'Well, I knew where it was leading, but Eliza tossed her head and said she didn't care. She said she liked him and she was so sick of her life in the mill with all the racket and smells and them wool fibres blowing everywhere. She said he'd promised her a new life. A little cottage out of town in the fresh air, and not to have to work again. If she'd be his mistress.'

Oh, poor Eliza, thought Caroline. And poor Mother.

'Eliza never got that little cottage. As soon as she started with you, Caroline, she got ill. It was partly her condition and partly her lungs were filled with all the fumes and with the wool fluff blowing about in them devilish mills, so she was having difficulty breathing. She needed caring for. So, of course, she stayed here with me. I used to go out when he was due to come,' she said, her face grim. 'I blamed him for all her troubles even though he showered money on her like the rain as comes down from the sky.'

'Did you hate him?' Caroline asked in a low small voice.

'I sometimes felt I might do him violence for what he did to my sister,' Mary said grimly. 'He thought he was being kind, doing the right thing by everyone. But, oh, I think her heart was broken. You'll no doubt know your mother — Mrs Brooke — was sadly without a child. She didn't seem as if she'd carry one to the full term, nor keep it alive if she did. Anyway at the time Eliza told your father about her own condition, your mother had just lost another baby.'

'So,' Caroline broke in, 'he sent my mother away to her sister in London to recuperate from a miscarriage and then told Eliza he would bring her baby up as his own once it was born.'

'Yes. But it was worse than that. He made your mother swear never to tell a living soul about losing her own baby. He let folks think she was still with child. She went to Oxford to hide herself away. He made her stay until the last possible moment, then he sent for her to come back and he kept her like a prisoner in her room, so no-one would see her poor belly was flat and empty. Eliza begged him to let her keep you when you were born. But he wouldn't listen. He just kept telling her she'd never want for money, as long as she kept the secret.'

Caroline bowed her head. Oh Father, Father!

'And when you were born, the midwife took you away, bundled in her cloak, when you were only a few hours old. And Eliza didn't last more than a few weeks afterwards. She'd lost a lot of blood, you see, at the birth. And her lungs were all furred up and scarred from all those years working in the mills.'

'Oh, Mary, I am so, so sorry!' Caroline burst out, wretched and miserable. 'Does anyone else know this secret?' she whispered.

'No. The husband I had then died a year later. My present husband knows nothing. Your secret's safe with me.'

Caroline took her hand. 'Might I come to see you again? And soon?'

'I shall be extremely vexed if you don't.'

'And will you come to Brackenfield?' Caroline asked wistfully. 'To visit me?'

'I don't know. I've never been anywhere so grand.' Mary gave her niece an arch look. 'I'm not sure if I want to be playing the poor relation. We're not paupers, you know. My husband has a good job as a mill overseer.'

As they spoke, the door burst open and a woman came in, her loud wails filling the room.

'Rosie Higgins!' Mary exclaimed. 'What's the matter?'

'My Jack's to be thrown out of work. There's new machines coming. We're ruined. We'll all starve, him and me and the little children.' She threw her apron over her head and howled.

'There, there, he'll get new work elsewhere,' Mary soothed.

'No. The mill master won't give him a recommendation. He says Jack's too old, but he's still strong and willing to do owt that comes along. Oh, dear Lord, what is to become of us?'

Mary held the weeping woman close against her, her eyes seeking Caroline's and ruefully indicating that she should leave.

As she walked to her carriage Caroline was shaken with a torrent of feelings and failed to register a man's brisk departure from a house close to Mary's. But when he almost collided with her in his haste she was astonished to see that it was Edward Seymour. 'Mr Seymour, sir!' she exclaimed.

He too was disconcerted, his brows drawing together in a dark frown. Immediately he regained his urbane manner. 'Miss Brooke! What in heaven's name brings you to these parts?'

'I have been visiting the family of a former employee of my father's,' she said swiftly.

'Indeed. I am surprised that a lady such as yourself should be troubled with such matters and I must warn you to take the greatest care when walking here on your own,' Seymour remonstrated. 'There are many ruffians and villains about.'

'I shall take good care, sir,' she said with quiet composure. 'My carriage is waiting at the end of the street.'

'I am glad to hear it, Miss Brooke. I shall hand you into it personally.'

As they walked along together, Caroline considered taking the opportunity to ask Seymour's advice on mantraps, then suddenly realised she had no wish to seek his advice on anything at all. She saw now how his charm was shallow and his offers of help faintly intimidating.

The calm, strong integrity of Robert Parker flashed suddenly across her mind, awakening new sensations. A warm flush crept into her face as she admitted to herself that her admiration for Robert Parker had been steadily growing.

She was pensive during the drive back to Brackenfield, concerned that Robert might have found her cold when she parted from him after their ride back from Fir Tree Lodge. She wished she could see him again to explain herself. And then it occurred to her that she could never explain herself, not if she wanted to guard her shocking secret.

6

Robert had spent a considerable part of the morning supervising the packing of several dozen bales of cloth which were to go to a clothing manufacturer in Derbyshire. As the last wagon rolled away through the gates he saw a smart barouche turn in and draw up on the cobbles outside his house.

A man got out then offered his hand to help a lady step down. Robert did not recall seeing them before. They were dressed in the latest fashion and the lady had a queenly and imperious air.

'May I help you?' he asked. 'I am Robert Parker, master of Parker Mill.'

The lady spoke. 'Good day, sir. I am Mrs Markham, and this is my husband, Mr David Markham.'

Mr Markham nodded and bowed. Neither husband nor wife smiled.

'I am the daughter of Mr Jacobson, Cloth Merchant,' Mrs Markham said. 'I have to give you the sad news that my father died last week. And I would wish to speak with you on matters of finance.'

Her hard, meaningful stare sent a chill into Robert's blood as he guided the couple into his house.

Seating herself in one of the chairs in Robert's sitting-room, Mrs Markham came straight to the point. 'You obtained a loan from my father recently,' she said, making it sound like an accusation. 'My husband has the details.'

Mr Markham unfolded a sheaf of papers and spread them over his lap.

'A considerable sum,' Mrs Markham said.

'Yes, ma'am. And at a considerable rate of interest,' Robert remarked.

'And there was a previous loan, whose payments run conjointly with the more recent one? Is that correct, Mr Parker?'

'That is correct,' he said quietly. 'As you will no doubt also know, ma'am, the agreed payments have all been made on time. And as business matters are going well for me at present, I am confident of being able to discharge the debt in full within the two year period stipulated in the agreement.'

Mrs Markham appeared unimpressed. 'I am my father's only surviving child and he has left the whole of his fortune to me. My husband and I are not at all happy that our money should be tied up in loans. We have financial needs of our own.' Her cold eyes bored into Robert's face. 'We have come to call in the loan, Mr Parker.'

Robert had already guessed as much. His mind was racing through the implications of the Markham's request.

'What is your answer, sir?' Mrs Markham demanded sharply.

'If you are considering a full repayment of the loan within the next few weeks, then I am afraid I shall have great difficulty in obliging you.'

'It is not a question of obliging us,' Mrs Markham responded, 'it is a question of your finding ways and means to deliver the money due to us. Within the next month.'

'That is not possible,' Robert said evenly.

'I am sure you are aware sir, that the agreement you signed with my father stipulated that the loan could be called in at any time, at the request of the financier?'

'I am, indeed, ma'am. But there was a verbal understanding between Mr Jacobson and myself that such a measure would only be taken in exceptional circumstances. For example if my business should fail — which is not the case.'

Mrs Markham's face was like a stone. 'If you are not able to raise the money due to my husband and myself, then we shall have no alternative but to possess your house and the mill.'

'I must ask you to reconsider your request,' Robert told the couple. 'I can assure you that the loan repayments will continue to be made regularly.'

'We don't doubt that, sir,' Mrs Markham responded sharply. 'However, we have pressing financial needs of our own. And we require capital, not income. That is it in a nutshell.'

They are wanting to buy a grand house and land, thought Robert. There was no hope of changing their minds.

'Would you at least give me a few days to consider my position?' he asked.

Mrs Markham frowned. 'We have stated everything quite clearly. You either agree to pay us the money, or we take possession of the house and the mill. We need an answer now.'

'It is normal business procedure to allow a period of consideration, my dear,' Mr Markham observed mildly.

'Oh, David!' Mrs Markham exclaimed, scowling in anger at her husband.

'Given a little time, my love, Mr Parker might be able to think of ways to pay us the money, so that we do not have the trouble and expense of possessing his buildings, and attempting to re-sell them.'

Mrs Markham pouted and huffed. 'Oh, very well.'

'Shall we say two weeks from today,' Mr Markham suggested, rising to his feet. 'If we do not hear from you by then, we will call again, Mr Parker. This same day, at this same time.'

He held the door for his wife, who hurried through with a swish of silk skirts.

Robert stood stunned and motionless in the hall, listening until the sounds of the departing barouche's wheels had faded into silence.

Edward Seymour put his horse into a gallop and raced towards Brackenfield hell for leather.

He had been considering calling on Caroline Brooke for some time, with the possibility of making an offer of marriage even though he was not entirely sure that he was ready to give up the freedom of his bachelor state. There was a very pretty lady in London whom he had been consoling for the misfortune of being married to a very rich, old and ugly man, and the liaison was still going strong.

As Laidlaw answered the door and showed him in, Seymour tossed him his visiting card. 'Be good enough to see if Miss Brooke will receive me,' he said curtly.

Caroline was standing beside the fireplace, wearing a gown fashioned from some soft material in a shade of delicate dove-grey. Her face was slightly flushed. She is all of a flutter to see me, Seymour thought, gratified. He went to stand close to her.

'Miss Brooke, Caroline. There is a very important matter on which I wish to speak with you.'

She looked disappointingly calm. 'Yes?'

'I'm sure you must, by now, be aware of my high regard for you. You seem to me the embodiment of all that is beautiful and graceful in a woman. And I flatter myself that you are not indifferent to me.'

Caroline dropped her head.

'My dear Caroline,' he said, adopting a low, reverent tone. 'Will you please do me the great honour of giving me your hand in marriage?'

There was a long silence. Seymour became uneasy. 'Miss Brooke!' he prompted. 'I made you an offer of marriage. Is it possible to give me an answer?'

'Yes,' she murmured. 'Yes, I heard you Mr Seymour. And — I can't marry you. I am sorry.'

'What?' He was thunderstruck. 'But why?'

She gave a long sigh. 'I am truly sorry,' she repeated.

'That is no answer!' he countered heatedly, his pretty speechifying all going by the board. 'Is there someone else?' he demanded. 'Another man who has claimed your affections?' He stopped, a terrible suspicion stealing into his mind. 'Surely not that Parker fellow!' Jealousy roared through him at the very thought.

Her face flooded with colour. 'No,' she said softly.

He struggled to control his fury. 'You have made your position quite plain, Miss Brooke,' he informed her coldly. 'I hope you will forgive me for taking up your time. I wish you good-day.'

As Caroline watched him stride from the room, she covered her face with her hands. There seemed to be a storm raging in her mind and her body. She could never love Edward Seymour. And not only because she had had her eyes opened to certain aspects of his character, but because she had gradually come to understand her growing feelings for Robert Parker. But those feelings of regard and love must never be expressed, and could never be consummated.

She could not even presume to ask for his advice on the matter of the man traps and the desperate situation of Rosie Higgins and her family, even though she longed for the comfort of his help and opinion. She felt as though her worth as a woman was steadily sinking. Not only could she no longer look forward to a happy marriage with a good man, but she was condemned to a life of secrecy and evasions.

Meanwhile Edward Seymour, galloping away from Brackenfield in a fury, was now convinced that Caroline had rejected him because of some secret regard for that damnable fellow Parker. The pink flush on her cheeks had spoken volumes. The notion of Parker getting his hands on the Brooke fortune was unbearable to contemplate. Rage boiled within him. And it did not take Seymour long to decide on the most effective way of striking back at Robert Parker.

It was now two weeks since the Markhams' visit to Parker Mill, and it was with a sense of foreboding that Robert heard the sound of the wheels of their barouche coming into the yard at midday.

They had brought along an accounting clerk whom they had engaged to draw up an inventory of the mill and all its contents and assets. After that he was to go into Robert's house and repeat the exercise.

Robert could not refrain from making a fresh appeal. 'I have been considering my financial position,' he told the couple, 'and I am confident I could pay you back a quarter of the loan within the next week.'

Mr Markham looked suspicious. 'You led us to believe you had very few liquid assets when we last spoke. How is that now you are suddenly able to offer such a large sum?'

'Because I have decided that it would be better to sell certain family treasures than risk losing my mill and my house,' Robert replied evenly.

'What treasures are these?' Mrs Markham asked.

'Some pieces of French furniture from the early part of the last century, ma'am. They belonged to my grandparents.'

Mrs Markham glanced at her husband. 'I think I should see these items. I might well favour the French style when we come to furnishing our new house.'

Mr Markham sighed. 'If you wish, my dear.'

'You go and accompany the clerk in the mill to ensure that all is above board,' she told her husband. 'Mr Parker will show me to his house and point out the items mentioned.'

Holding tight to his patience, Robert led the way to his house. As they crossed the yard, he saw another carriage pull up at the gates. He stood watching as the driver sprang down and opened the door. And then his heart gave a thrill of shock as Caroline Brooke, with Freddie in her arms, stepped out and glanced hesitantly around her.

'Please excuse me for a moment,' he said to Mrs Markham. He walked forward and unlocked the gates to allow Caroline and her maid Susan to pass through.

'Miss Brooke!' he said softly, unable

138

to conceal his delight at seeing her.

'Please forgive me for calling unannounced, but I was on the way back from some errands in the town, and I very much wanted to ask your advice on some business matters.' Her words came tumbling out, and as she spoke her cheeks grew pink.

'I am delighted to see you, Miss Brooke,' he said simply. His eyes connected with hers for a moment, and he was suddenly convinced that there was a shared attraction between them. That she had some true feeling for him, not simply as an advisor, or a friend. But as a man.

Caroline was looking towards the house, sensing the presence of an onlooker. 'Oh!' she exclaimed, spotting Mrs Markham. 'Am I intruding on an engagement?'

'No, not at all. The lady and her husband called unexpectedly on a matter relating to the mill.'

Robert showed Caroline and her maid into the sitting-room and then invited Mrs Markham to inspect whatever she liked of the contents of his house, making it quite clear by his expression that the front room was most definitely out of bounds.

'Well, really, Mr Parker!' Mrs Markham exclaimed. 'I would have thought that the important business discussions planned for today would take precedence over more dalliance with young ladies.'

'You are quite mistaken, ma'am,' Robert said curtly. 'Miss Brooke is a good friend who has come to consult me on business matters. You may look around my house at your leisure. If there are any items you wish to purchase that would enable me to discharge my debt sufficiently to put a halt to your vulture-like proceedings, then kindly let me know.' He returned to the sitting-room, ignoring Mrs Markham's exclamation of outrage.

Caroline was sitting on a small sofa by the window, trying to look as though she had not heard anything of what had been going on in the hall, although it

140

was impossible that she could have missed the hard words and raised voices.

As Robert entered she murmured to Susan to wait outside in the hall for a few minutes.

Robert sat down opposite her. To be in her presence sent joy spinning through him. 'How may I assist you, Miss Brooke?'

Hesitantly she told him of her doubts about sanctioning a man trap to be installed on her estate. 'What is your opinion, Mr Parker?' she asked, her blue eyes filled with anxiety.

He smiled. 'That you tell your gamekeeper that man traps are sadistic, inhuman contraptions and should have been outlawed years ago. And that it is out of the question to install one at Brackenfield.'

Caroline stared at him. 'It's as simple as that?'

'Certainly. It's been my experience that employees welcome firm direction as long as the motives behind them are based on sound principles.'

'Yes, I see,' she said slowly. 'Thank you for that, Mr Parker.' She paused, hesitating. 'There is something else. I have personal knowledge of a mill worker who is to be thrown out of work because of the new machines. His poor wife is in despair. It seems to me so hard and cruel for people who are honest and hardworking to have all they have strived for suddenly taken from them.' She stopped.

'It is a matter which worries me constantly,' Robert agreed. 'But you see, if we mill manufacturers fail to take advantage of the new inventions we will be unable to compete for orders. Our trade will dwindle to nothing. And then all of the workers would lose their means of earning a living.'

She fiddled agitatedly with one of her pearl earrings which eventually became dislodged and fell unnoticed on to the sofa. 'I understand that. But my heart tells me, that as a woman, I have to think of the wives and children who suffer from no fault of their own.

'Imagine it, Mr Parker! Little children who have nothing to eat.'

Robert was so affected by the depth of her tender, womanly concern that he found it difficult not to sweep her into his arms and hold her close to him.

'I have not grown up blinkered and ignorant,' Caroline told him. 'I have always known that other people were not as fortunate as myself. But I didn't meet those people, I knew nothing of their hearts and minds. It is only when you actually meet one of those unfortunate souls that you truly understand their hardship — and reflect that if God had arranged things differently, it might have been you.'

Robert sensed some deep undercurrent running beneath her words. Something intensely private and personal. 'What can I do to help?' he asked Caroline quietly.

'The family are called Higgins,' she told him. 'The man is a hard worker, but not young any more. They have three children. If he doesn't get work soon they will have to sell all their goods, and eventually they will face starvation.'

'If he is a good honest workman, he could well get work of some kind,' Robert ventured.

'Perhaps. But his mill master will not agree to give him a written recommendation, and that will surely make things difficult for him.' She looked straight into Robert's eyes.

'Were you hoping that I might be able to offer Higgins a post?' he prompted gently.

'Yes.' She smiled with relief. 'Oh, Mr Parker, I have been so worried about asking you this favour. I thought you might think I was just meddling, and that you would be angry.'

'I do need a man to help in the boiler house,' Robert reflected, whilst grimly reminding himself that he might soon not need any workmen at all. 'He'd need to be able to withstand a good deal of heat and steam.' He stopped, not wanting to trouble Caroline with the threat hanging over the mill.

'Oh, but Rosie — that's his wife — says that Jack would take anything and be grateful for it,' Caroline exclaimed, her eyes shining with pleasure.

Robert turned as there was a sharp rapping on the door. Freddie, who was curled on the floor at Caroline's feet, sprang up growling.

'Mr Parker!' came Mrs Markham's imperious tones, 'I need to speak with you. Immediately.'

Robert sighed, wishing Freddie could be temporarily transformed into a bull mastiff with huge fangs.

'Would you excuse me for a moment,' he said to Caroline, rising.

'Yes, of course,' she said. 'Mr Parker, I can see that you are busy. Perhaps I should leave now.'

'No, please stay, Miss Brooke. I shall not keep you waiting long.'

Mrs Markham assailed him in the hallway. 'There is nothing of interest to me amongst your furniture and ornaments,' she told him with disdain. 'And, thinking it over, it's my opinion that the Italian style will soon displace the French and become all the new rage.' She flung open the front door and stepped outside, almost colliding with her husband who was making for the house, followed by the clerk.

'We have completed an initial inventory of the mill and its fittings,' Mr Markham observed.

Robert decided to make one final appeal to the Markhams. 'I am sure we could come to some mutually satisfactory agreement regarding the repayment of the loan. I cannot pay you back all of the money instantly, but I can promise to find ways of reimbursing you much sooner than the original agreement stipulated.'

'Gentlemen's agreements are no use to me,' Mrs Markham broke in. 'We shall press on with the possession of your material assets.'

From the corner of his vision Robert noticed Caroline walk from the house, her eyes seeking his. When she saw that he was engaged with the Markhams, she politely stopped a few yards away, occupying herself with fondling Freddie.

'Please go ahead with whatever you wish to do,' Robert instructed the Markhams. 'If you wish to take the clerk through the house, then do so.' He turned and went to join Caroline.

She looked up at him. 'Are you in trouble?' she asked, her voice low with concern.

'Yes. I was hoping to keep it from you.'

'Why? I am human, Mr Parker. I hope you don't think I shy away from life's difficulties.'

'Of course not.'

'Then tell me what is wrong?'

He shook his head. His throat felt full up. He could not talk here with workmen going to and fro, and the danger of the Markhams springing from the house and buttonholing him.

She laid her gloved fingers lightly on

his arm. 'Freddie needs some exercise. I was thinking of walking through the fields with him.' Her glance was inviting and expectant. She turned, gesturing to Susan to follow her.

'Then shall we walk together?' he suggested, delighted at her sensitivity to his discomfiture.

When they were safely out of earshot of the mill, she turned to him. 'Those people are not customers are they?'

'No.'

'Nor traders in raw materials?'

'They are money-lenders,' he said in a low voice.

'Oh!'

He could tell she was shocked. 'I doubt that you or your family will have had much use for the breed.' He smiled.

'No. I believe my father set up Brackenfield Mill with money from inheritances. Both he and my mother were fortunate to inherit from their parents and also other relatives.' She suddenly stumbled on a piece of rough ground and Robert reached out a hand to steady her. She glanced up him, her eyes warm and trusting. Robert bent his arm and drew her hand through it.

'Tell me about the beginning of Parker Mill,' Caroline invited him.

'I started with a little capital left to me by my uncle, and built up from there,' Robert told her, going on to outline the steady growth of his business, and finishing with his dismay at finding his new machines in pieces on the mill floor when he returned from his first visit to Brackenfield. 'I had taken out a loan in order to help fund the purchase of those machines,' he explained to Caroline.

'And when they were destroyed I decided that I must either replace them immediately or stand and watch my business sink under the competition. The money lender made sure to protect his investment. He demanded the mill and my house as security, and I had no choice but to agree.'

'No, of course not,' she agreed

swiftly. 'My father always used to say that a businessman gained nothing if he risked nothing.'

'Did he?' Robert smiled. 'Well I took a very grave risk indeed. I knew that my money lender was a shrewd man who drove a hard bargain, but I also knew that he trusted me to make enough profit from the business to pay him back within a reasonable span of time.' He stopped, the enormity of what was happening to his lifetime's work suddenly hitting him afresh.

'Then what went wrong?' Caroline asked.

'The money lender died, and his daughter and her husband tell me they're worried about the safety of their investment. They've called in the loan. And I am unable to pay.'

'These dreadful people mean you to give up your mill?' Caroline exclaimed, stopping dead. 'To dismantle your business, and to take your house also?'

'I'm afraid so.'

'Oh, that is wicked!'

'It is simply a feature of life in trade, I'm sorry to say.'

'Oh, Mr Parker! The world is so unjust!' She stared up at him. 'You must not give up the mill. Or your business. It has been your life. It would hurt you dreadfully to lose it all. Oh, I can't bear to think of it.'

They stood facing each other, the little dog jumping up at them enquiringly. The irony of her own wealth compared with Robert's desperate need for money flashed through Caroline's mind.

Perhaps she could offer him a loan. Surely not all of her money was tied up until she married or became an old spinster. She gazed up at him. 'Oh, how I wish I could help you!'

'You're very kind, Miss Brooke, but I couldn't accept your help, it would be quite wrong of me to presume on your concern and generosity.'

Caroline's mind was working furiously. She could ask Mr Hattersley to draw up a loan agreement. It would all be done quite properly, and then Robert could go on working Parker Mill.

He smiled down at her and they turned to walk back to the house and the mill. 'You mustn't trouble yourself with this matter, Miss Brooke. I will do all I can to find some kind of solution of my own.'

'How helpless I feel.' She sighed.

They walked on. Robert felt drugged by her closeness and the sympathy he could sense beating within her for his situation.

Quite suddenly all anxiety, awkwardness and caution left him. He might be about to lose everything he had worked for, but he would not lose this opportunity to speak honestly to Caroline. Perhaps the last chance he would have to speak to her on an equal footing before his downfall and disgrace.

'Miss Brooke, there is something very important I must tell you. I know it's not the custom for men and women to speak freely of their affections, but I am going to dare to go against convention. I want you to know that I have never felt such a depth of tenderness, affection and longing for another woman.

'I love you, my dearest Miss Brooke, with all my heart. And if my situation had been different, I would have ended this interview by asking you to consider spending a lifetime at my side — as my wife.'

The words seemed to hang in the air after he had spoken them. He could hardly believe what he had done. For a moment he wanted to pluck the words back and ask her to forget them forever. How could she even contemplate marrying him, a man teetering on the brink of ruin?

And then he looked at her and saw that she seemed to be neither shocked nor offended. Her expression was one of sadness and a curious resignation.

He was reminded of the anxiety he sometimes saw on the face of his workpeople; a look of total submission to the trials that fate had ordained for them.

She reached up and touched his cheek with the tips of her fingers. 'I too have feelings of love,' she said with an ache of sweetness and longing in her voice. 'And if matters had been different for me, I would have accepted you with all my heart.'

Robert stared down at her and for a moment his heart flared with sudden joyous hope, but he was at a loss to understand what she was trying to convey to him.

He struggled to frame questions which would persuade her to tell him something of the troubles she was burdened with.

She shook her head in slow regret. 'I cannot say any more,' she told him softly, and beckoning to her maid, she turned and hurried away to her waiting coach.

7

Mr Hattersley settled in Mr Brooke's former study and viewed Caroline with an unctuous smile. 'You sent for me, dear madam — I am at your service. What is it you wish to speak with me about?'

Caroline began to recite the speech she had carefully rehearsed prior to this interview. 'I have a recommendation from a friend to make an investment that could be most profitable. I'd like you to advise me of how much ready money I might have at my disposal to do this.'

Mr Hattersley sighed. 'May I ask you to give me some details of this investment, Miss Brooke? What company is it you wish to invest in? What securities are available?'

Caroline had not anticipated such quizzing. She changed tack. 'Do I have any money available in addition to my yearly allowance?' she asked. 'I received legacies from both my mother and her aunt. I never needed to use the money. Where is it? Surely it is not locked away like my father's fortune.'

'I could investigate the situation,' Mr Hattersley told her cautiously. 'But I must repeat, Miss Brooke, I am not at all happy about this *investment* you wish to make. There are so many unprincipled rascals about these days, only too ready to relieve an unsuspecting lady of her money.'

Caroline began to see the hopelessness of persuading him. 'Very well, I will be honest with you, Mr Hattersley. I have a worthy business friend who is in trouble and requires a loan. I have absolute faith in his integrity and his resolve to pay me back in full with adequate interest. I was hoping you would draw up a suitable document regarding a loan agreement.'

'Miss Brooke!' he exclaimed, shaking his head. 'You would not believe how many ladies I have had to rescue from the blandishments of unscrupulous men. And just imagine the horror your late dear father would have felt, to think of a daughter of his, a lady of quality, offering money to a man.'

Caroline winced. Of course, Mr Hattersley was quite right. She had known that all along, and it was simply her desire to help Robert which had overridden her usual judgement.

Frustrated by her inability to help Robert financially, Caroline found some comfort in stuffing a purse with money and taking it to Mary Bracegirdle who would pass it on to Rosie Higgins the next time she called.

'You've a truly kind heart,' Mary told her. 'Like your mother.' She stroked Caroline's cheek.

'When will you come to see me at Brackenfield, Aunt Mary?' Caroline asked.

'Now then, who can say? When I've learned to be a grand enough lady not to disgrace you with my rough and ready ways.'

Caroline hugged Mary close. She knew it would take a good deal of time and patience to persuade the proud Mrs Bracegirdle that she had as much right to visit Brackenfield as her niece did to drink tea at 8 Alfred Street. She was willing to wait.

After leaving Mary, she instructed the driver to take her to Parker Mill. As they approached the mill Caroline's heart began to beat with apprehension and excitement. She had the excuse of the loss of a pearl earring as a genuine reason to visit. But she had to admit that the main motive behind this delicate mission was simply to see Robert again even though there was no future in their regard for each other.

As her coach driver reined the horses to a halt she saw that the gates to the mill yard were flung open. The workers were streaming out; a host of men, women and children, laughing and jesting.

Robert was in the yard, supervising the unloading of wrapped bales from a sturdy wagon. He saw her instantly as she walked towards the gates and came forward to meet her.

'Miss Brooke!' His eyes were alight with feeling.

'I believe I lost an earring when I last visited,' she told him. 'It's a small grey pearl one my mother gave to me.' She stared up at him, drinking in every line of his strong, sensitive face.

'Of course. Where do you think the earring was lost?'

Her throat had gone quite dry. 'In the sitting-room I think.'

He led the way into his house. Caroline walked ahead into the sitting-room, gesturing to her maid Susan to wait in the hallway.

'You were sitting here, beside the window, I believe,' Robert said, running his hands between the seat and back of the sofa. 'Ah!' He straightened up smiling, the pearl between his fingers.

'Oh! I'm so pleased to have it back.' She was at a loss what to say next.

'Miss Brooke,' he said gently, touching her arm, propelling her towards him. 'I realise that you were distressed when we spoke together last time. I feared I had spoken out of turn. But I have not forgotten your final words to me that day.' He paused. 'May I not hope? Unworthy as I am.'

'Oh, Mr Parker,' she said, her voice husky. 'You are more than worthy! But there is no hope.' Tears sprang into her eyes. 'I cannot agree to be your wife, Robert.'

He put his arms around her and held her close as she wept.

Eventually she became calmer. 'There is no fault on your side, Robert,' she told him. 'If things were different for me, nothing would make me happier than to be your wife.'

He looked at her mystified, wretched at being unable to ease her distress.

She made a valiant attempt to smile. 'I would like to return to Brackenfield now,' she said. Her tone was soft, yet determined. He sensed that she was distancing herself from him. Becoming once more the wealthy and respected mistress of Brackenfield. 'Would you take me to my carriage?'

'Of course.' His heart beat thick with love as she dabbed her eyes.

As they walked out into the yard he noticed that the weather had turned cloudy as though a grey roof had lowered itself over the moors. Rain splattered the cobbles. The yard was now deserted, the mill gates locked.

Suddenly a gunshot split the air. Caroline's body jerked in alarm.

'Dear God!' murmured Robert.

'What is it?' she whispered, her hand grasping his arm.

'An attack, I fear.'

'Machine breakers?'

'More than likely.'

The shots were growing louder. There was the sound of steadily tramping feet.

Robert groaned internally. If only he had got Caroline into her carriage five minutes earlier she would now have been out of danger and safely on her way home.

A moving mass of men began to crowd against the gates.

'You must go back into the house,' Robert told Caroline with quiet urgency.

'Oh, Robert!' said Caroline, standing her ground. 'What will happen? What are you going to do?'

'I shall speak to them.'

She shook her head. Fear was tearing through her nerves, but she could not move. It was unthinkable to hide herself away and leave Robert to the mercy of this menacing group.

'Mr Parker, we've come to break up all your steam machines,' a voice called out. 'Before you send us working people to starvation.' There were more shouts. Another shot rang out.

'It is my hope that there will be no men or women from my mill who will face starvation,' Robert called out in firm, carrying tones, but his words were greeted with howls of derision.

There was the noise of clanging

metal. Caroline saw with horror that two of the men were hacking at the locks of the gates with fierce looking iron tools.

A chant went up. 'We're coming in, we're coming in.'

The noise sounded to Caroline like the baying of foxhounds who had caught a scent. 'Oh, it is like the hunt!' she exclaimed, looking up at Robert with terror stricken eyes.

'Go inside the house,' Robert urged her. 'Caroline, please go now.'

She swallowed. Again she shook her head. It was not that she had any desire to go against his wishes. She simply could not walk away and leave him to this wild, crazed mob, even though the fear was washing over her in great horrifying waves.

The gates were proving more resilient than the mob had envisaged. Frustrated, one or two men picked up stones from the road and began to hurl them at the broad front of the mill.

A man at the front of the rabble who

had been noisily urging the others on, let out a howl of glee as one of the windows smashed and fragments of glass shattered on the cobbles.

Caroline felt her ears ringing with the noise of the growing volley of stones. Splinters of glass were everywhere now. A flying shard struck her on the temple, drawing a sheet of blinding light before her eyes. Her knees buckled. She sank down.

Robert caught her and held her in his arms. Looking into the crowd he blazed out at them: 'You do well, my friends, hurling stones and hurting a helpless woman who has never done any harm to anyone. Your only wish is to destroy and to commit violence. You are cowards, all of you. Men who can only speak with the help of guns and iron bars. I pity and despise you, every single one of you.'

A deathly silence had fallen. The men working at the locks of the gate laid down their crowbars.

'My first task is to carry this poor

woman to the safety of my house,' Robert told them. 'You may break down the gates while I am away. Do what you want. Set fire to the mill, and when I return, kill me if that is what will satisfy you.'

There was not a sound. The communal rage of the men behind the gates had vanished like a fire doused with cold water. Their eyes were all on the pale upturned face of the woman lying in Robert's arms. A thin ribbon of blood was threading its way into her hairline. Her cheeks were as white and still as marble. Tears stood on the end of her long lashes.

Robert carried her to the entrance of the house, and finding the door firmly closed, propped her gently against the wooden doorframe.

The men shuffled their feet, involuntarily moving back from the gates. They looked towards their leader, the hooded, cloaked man who had urged them on without ever saying a word or casting a stone himself. He grasped one of the retreating men. 'Stand your ground!'

The quitter shook himself free. There was a scuffle. In a gesture of anger and desperation the man grasped at the concealing hood of the leader's cloak and wrenched it back, so that it fell to his shoulders. The cloaked man made a futile attempt to hide his face, then flung up his bared head in bold defiance.

Robert gasped as recognition swept through him.

The man leading the rabble was no pitiful, displaced worker driven to desperate acts in the face of starvation. It was Edward Seymour.

Robert felt his body shake with rage. 'Seymour!' he breathed. 'You take it on yourself to exert your selfish brutal will to incite a bunch of poor ignorant ruffians to come here and commit acts of violence.'

There was a deathly silence. Seymour made no response, staring stonily ahead.

'You have no interest in the cause of the workers,' Robert went on, gaining a swift grasp on the other man's motivation. 'You simply use them for your own purposes, persuade them to follow you like sheep and goad them on until blood is shed.' He glanced with concern at Caroline's limp body resting against the doorframe. 'Neither had you any thought or compassion for that innocent woman. A woman who you know as a friend. I feel nothing but contempt for you, sir.'

The men around Seymour slowly dropped back from him, shifting their feet and looking uneasy. Seymour was soon isolated, standing facing Robert on his own.

Robert saw a number of conflicting expressions move across Seymour's features. He doubted that he saw real remorse, but there was certainly dismay at having no more cards to play.

'I suppose you realise the damage I could do to your reputation, sir, if I were to make it known amongst the manufacturers and landowners of Bradford that Mr Seymour of Kershaw Hall was amusing himself encouraging rebels and Luddites. Provoking violence and endangering life.'

'You must do as you wish, sir,' Seymour responded, his face blank.

'It would not be difficult for me to set this mob against you,' Robert told Seymour softly. 'Men who have lost their livelihood and whose children face starvation are not difficult to persuade. And, I assure you, I know a good deal more about their hopes and fears than you.'

A twist of fear distorted Seymour's urbane features.

'If I were to tell these men that you have no sympathy whatsoever with their plights, that in fact you look down on them as poor wretches whom fate has decreed should labour and suffer so that idle men might enjoy more creature comforts, I fear they wouldn't cling very long to their loyalty towards you.'

'You would not do it, Parker,' breathed Seymour. 'Because you are too damned noble and tender-hearted.'

'I am a mill master,' Robert reminded him. 'I have not spent years managing working men without learning how to enforce order and the need to stand firm.'

Just at this moment there were a number of low growls of discontent from the waiting crowd and Robert saw Seymour's adam's apple bob as he tried to swallow his growing apprehension.

'If I were to expose you as a fork-tongued hypocrite,' Robert continued, 'I think these followers of yours could soon take on the role of hounds on the scent of a fox.'

The growls from the bored, thwarted men excluded from this conversation were now increasing.

'Very well,' Seymour told Robert, hurriedly. 'I admit it. I've been amusing myself for some time consorting with friends in low places, and I brought this rabble here especially to cause trouble for you. You've been getting too big for your boots, Parker, presuming to insinuate yourself into the favours of a woman of quality.'

'Actions motivated by jealousy and revenge rarely have a satisfactory outcome,' Robert said thoughtfully, as he observed Seymour's unease he found his own power to destroy the other man monetarily heady and intoxicating. He knew he must resist it.

'Leave my premises Seymour,' he told him, with calm authority. 'Leave and take your *supporters* with you. If you go now I give you my promise that I will never say a word of this to anyone.'

Relief flooded Seymour's face. 'Very well, but before I go, I'd like you to know that this is the first and the last time I shall ever get myself mixed up in such grubby, shabby proceedings.'

'Is this truly the first time?' Robert cut in sharply. 'What about the night of the January raid on my mill? You and I were both dining at Brackenfield, weren't we? But maybe you were the absent architect of the incident?'

Seymour's lip curled. 'I had nothing whatever to do with the earlier raid on your mill, Parker. The ins and outs of your wretched machines have never been of any interest to me whatsoever.'

'I believe you,' Robert said. 'The men who visited me that night knew what they were doing. I doubt this sorry band you brought along would achieve very much even if they managed to storm the gates.'

He stepped forward and called out to the waiting men. 'Stand back. Make a space for Mr Seymour to pass through.'

Seymour's previous fear was replaced with smiling insolence. 'You have an unhappy knack of getting the better of me, Parker. But I know when to beat a dignified retreat. And how I long to return to London and civilisation. I have always loathed this cold, God-forsaken place.'

Without so much as a further glance at Caroline, he turned on his heel. Pushing his way through the clump of men who had remained to support him, he strode off.

Robert carefully raised Caroline to her feet. 'Can you stand?' he asked anxiously. 'Lean against me.'

'It is just a graze,' she said, raising a trembling hand to her face.

The watching men made a low groan of sympathy on her behalf. With a final glance at Robert's grim face they turned, their wish for retreat suddenly urgent. Within seconds they had all vanished.

'Oh, thank heaven, they've gone, and you are safe,' she exclaimed to Robert, sinking against him and closing her eyes again. He caught her as she was about to fall and carried her to the house.

Susan was waiting in the doorway. 'Oh, Miss Brooke, shall I get the doctor?'

'No,' murmured Caroline. 'I will soon be well.'

'I'll go prepare some hot sweet tea,' Susan said, hurrying away to the kitchen.

Robert carried Caroline into the drawing-room and laid her gently on the sofa. He took out a handkerchief and began to stroke the blood from her forehead. 'Oh, Caroline, I love you so very much. Pray God you will soon be yourself again, my dearest.'

Caroline still felt dizzy and faint, but her senses were beginning to come alive again. She became aware of Robert's presence and that it was his hand which was administering the reviving caresses. She gave a faint smile and began to struggle into a sitting position. She touched the site of the wound. 'It is not much at all.' She began to look anxious and hunted. 'Robert, I must go home. I mustn't take up your time . . .'

'Take up my time! My dearest Caroline, you may take all of the time I have left to me, and it still wouldn't be enough,' he said, smiling at the extravagance of his words.

'No,' she moaned. 'No, it can't be.' She turned her head away, and there was a long, beating pause.

He placed his hands around her face and tilted her chin so that she was forced to meet his eyes. 'What can't be, my sweetest?'

'Marriage. An alliance between us. I cannot marry you, Robert.'

'And I cannot accept your refusal,' he said. 'I truly believe that you love me, as I love you.'

'Yes! Oh, yes, I do!'

'Then why will you not marry me?'

She stared at him. 'I cannot marry anyone. Any gentleman, that is.'

He frowned. 'Dear God. Why not? Tell me, dearest. You mustn't keep anything back from me. You must trust me. I have to know what is troubling you so much.'

'I cannot. I only recently made the discovery myself. The shock of it was terrible. For a time I thought my life was over. But I cannot tell you — you will no longer love me,' she said.

'That is not so. I shall still love you whatever it is that is troubling you. Now tell me!' he commanded sternly. 'You may tell me anything at all. I will not be shocked. And I will not reject you.' He said nothing more. He set his face into immovable lines and made it plain that he would not give in until she yielded up her secret.

'My father betrayed my mother,' she said, her eyes cast down. 'He took a girl at Brackenfield Mill for his mistress. And when she had a child he made her give it up so that he could have it brought up as his own legitimate child.' She let out a long sigh. 'And that child was me.'

Robert gave himself time to absorb the impact of the words. Then he leaned forwards, took her in his arms and pressed a warm, firm kiss on her lips.

'I am the illegitimate child of a girl who spent most of her life working at the looms in Bradford's mills,' Caroline whispered. 'Her blood flows in my veins. The blood of a humble working girl.'

'And is that shameful? To have a

mother who earned her bread by honest toil?'

'No. But it is not a fitting background for the wife of a man like yourself, Robert. A man who has prospects before him. A man who will need powerful connections to help him along in his business. The people who hold that power are proud. Do you want to be fastened to a wife whose mother would be scorned by your friends and associates if they found out about her?'

'But they never will. This part of your past will be something we shall treasure and share only with each other.'

'Even so,' she protested, 'even if the matter isn't public, I still carry a burden of shame in my blood. And the guilt of it, now that my father is dead, is mine alone.'

'In my eyes, you carry no guilt,' Robert told her. 'I love you for yourself, for your sweetness and your courage and your generous heart. I think of you simply as Caroline, the woman I love with all my heart. The woman I want to

176

spend the rest of my life with.'

He paused, smoothing the curls around her face. 'And the woman I want to be the mother of my children. Do you think I love you for your wealth or your birth? Do you really consider me such a grasping, vain person to be swayed by the opinion of those who place status and riches above human bonds?'

She stared at him for a long, suspenseful moment. 'No,' she said at last. 'I am sorry that I ever believed that of you Robert. Will you forgive me?'

He made a show of considering. 'It is possible,' he murmured, lowering his head to hers, 'that I could be persuaded to be lenient . . . '

A delicious silence followed. When Susan came in with the tea, she set the tray down softly on the table and crept noiselessly away.

In the last weeks of that year, Caroline and Robert were married in the church in whose hallowed ground her father was buried.

The months prior to the wedding had been a joyful time for them both. Shortly after the announcement of their betrothal in the national newspapers Mr and Mrs Markham had turned up at Parker Mill bowing and scraping. What a delight to hear of his alliance with Miss Brooke. What a pleasure to receive a letter from her lawyer announcing the happy couple's intention of a prompt settlement of the loan once they were married.

Mr Derby too had changed his tune, promptly making known his readiness to stand down as the appointed guardian of Brackenfield Mill. He had invited Robert to a lavish lunch at his country house to discuss the issue of the handover.

'He was most cordial,' Robert told Caroline. 'My status seems to have risen remarkably now I'm to be the husband of the respected heiress Miss Caroline Brooke and future master of Brackenfield. His words, not mine.'

Their regard and love for each other

had grown steadily over the months. Whilst the prospect of Caroline's wealth had eased Robert's worries about Parker Mill, he was able to respond to her anxieties attached to Brackenfield Mill and the estate, quietly dealing with troubling matters if that was what she wished.

And Aunt Hilda had been delighted to hear that her niece was at last heeding her good advice to take a husband. Caroline and Robert had talked at length about sharing the secret of Caroline's birth with her much-loved aunt. Caroline had been torn and undecided.

She felt that Aunt Hilda's safe world and memories of her only brother could be tragically overturned by telling her the truth. But Robert thought that openness showed a greater trust and respect for Mrs Forsett which out-weighed all other considerations.

'But supposing her feelings for me were to change when she knows the truth,' Caroline protested biting her lip.

'You mustn't forget she is a lady of great respectability and propriety.'

'My feelings for you did not change,' he pointed out wryly. 'And I am moderately respectable.'

'Of course you are, dear Robert! But then as you often remind me, you are simply a foolish man who fell head over heels in love with a lady who tried to drive you away with her coldness and hostility. Why should I take notice of you?'

Robert had decided to abandon his efforts at counselling, and had pulled her down on to his knee and silenced her for some time.

Eventually Caroline was persuaded. One summer afternoon, whilst walking in the garden she had gently told Aunt Hilda about the secret letters which her father had hoped would never come to light. She told her the sad circumstances of her own birth and of Eliza's tragic early death.

The only detail she left out was her new closeness with her maternal aunt

Mary Bracegirdle; she did not feel Aunt Hilda could face that together with everything else.

Aunt Hilda had gone very quiet when told the news. Her face drained of its colour. 'So this is what has been troubling you!' she exclaimed. She took herself to the summerhouse in the far corner of the garden and sat on her own for a time. When she rejoined Caroline, she had a good deal to say.

'I always knew that your father had liaisons with girls from the mill. You see my dear, your mother was not strong and, if you will forgive my indelicacy, I think that she found a husband's attentions irksome. However I knew nothing of Eliza Bell. She was certainly not the first girl he had taken as a mistress, but she was clearly the last. And he must have had a very high regard for her if he was prepared to acknowledge her child.'

'I do believe that he did,' Caroline agreed.

'He was a proud man,' Aunt Hilda

continued. 'And although I would have expected him to support any child of an illicit liaison, I would never have expected him to adopt him or her as his own. He was not known for his warm feelings towards the working people, as you well know.'

Caroline thought once again of her father's last hours and how disturbed he had been by Robert's stubborn support of the workers. It suddenly occurred to her that he might have hated himself in his weakness in being attracted to poor working girls. And maybe Robert's remarks had awakened complex feelings of anger and renewed guilt. She would never know. And now, it did not matter. All that mattered was that her father had loved her dearly, and that she in turn adored her husband-to-be Robert.

'Yes, indeed he must have loved Eliza very much in his strange way,' Aunt Hilda decided. 'Arthur was never an easy man, you know, and he was such an odd mixture of arrogance and tenderness.' Tears sprang from her eyes.

I should not have told her, thought Caroline in distress.

Aunt Hilda was silent for a time. And then she took out her handkerchief and blew her nose. 'We must put the past behind us,' she said firmly. 'Nothing can change the fact that ever since I first held you as a tiny baby, I felt you were the daughter I would have wished to have if God had seen fit to give me one. I could not have wished for a better, more loving, more beautiful or wiser girl to love. You have been a shining light in my life, my dear. You always have been, and you always will be.'

Caroline put her arm around Aunt Hilda's shoulders and kissed her moist cheek.

'And as for this little matter we have talked of,' she concluded, waving her hand in a dismissive gesture, 'I never want to hear anything more about it. In fact as far as I am concerned I never even heard it at all! You have always been a perfect lady, my dear. Just like your dear mama, my sister-in-law. And nothing can ever alter that.'

They walked on a little. Aunt Hilda pointed out the buds on the roses and made a few suggestions as to how their flowering might be improved with the addition of a certain manure her own gardener had found excellent. Caroline had the sense that as far as her revelation was concerned, a forbidden book had been opened and very firmly shut.

'There is one more thing,' said Aunt Hilda. 'If I had a son, I think I would have been delighted if he had turned out as worthy and kind and strong as dear Robert. So you see Caroline, we can all look ahead to happy times and be merry and cheerful.'

On the day before the wedding Robert had his belongings moved to Brackenfield where he would officially take up residence after he and Caroline arrived home from their wedding tour.

As the newly-wed bride and groom

arrived back from the church to Brackenfield, the servants all ran out, waving and smiling and greeting. Freddie was there too, barking in excitement and making more noise than everyone else put together.

Laidlaw stepped forward. 'Welcome home, Mrs Parker,' he told his mistress gravely.

Carriages were rolling down the drive. Guests stepped out, their finery burnished by the deep gold of a setting winter sun.

Arm in arm Caroline and Robert walked back to the house to greet them.

THE END

We do hope that you have enjoyed reading this large print book.

Did you know that all of our titles are available for purchase?

We publish a wide range of high quality large print books including:
Romances, Mysteries, Classics
General Fiction
Non Fiction and Westerns

Special interest titles available in large print are:
The Little Oxford Dictionary
Music Book, Song Book
Hymn Book, Service Book

Also available from us courtesy of Oxford University Press:
Young Readers' Dictionary
(large print edition)
Young Readers' Thesaurus
(large print edition)

For further information or a free brochure, please contact us at:
Ulverscroft Large Print Books Ltd.,
The Green, Bradgate Road, Anstey,
Leicester, LE7 7FU, England.
Tel: (00 44) **0116 236 4325**
Fax: (00 44) **0116 234 0205**